A HEART WELL TRAVELED
VOLUME 2

A HEART WELL TRAVELED
VOLUME 2

EDITED BY SALLYANNE MONTI

SAPPHIRE BOOKS

SALINAS, CALIFORNIA

Preface

Magical, mystical, and otherworldly meets erotic, fanatical, and uncommon, in this supernatural assemblage of characters and uncanny plot twists. Each unique short story will take you on a long distance romantic journey through unusual love affairs across the miles, galaxies and time.

Is it fate, is it destiny, or is it an alternate reality flamed by fantasy?

Sallyanne Monti

Acknowledgment

A Heart Well Traveled Volume 2

This is Volume 2 in Sapphire Books' long distance romance anthology series, A Heart Well Traveled.

Earnest appreciation to this gifted group of lesbian authors, who placed the spirit of their creative bodies of work in our trust.

Sincere thanks to Ann McMan and TreeHouse Studios for the mystic cover art that brings the images of this project to life, and to LJ Reynolds for exceptional book design that accentuates the fast-paced nature of the stories.

Heartfelt thanks to Sapphire Books and Publisher Christine Svendsen, for dedication to literary excellence.

It's been a privilege to work in partnership to the shared realization of this distinctive literary collection.

Table of Contents

Living in Her Memories

By Vickie L. Adams

It started when I found an old photo album at a garage sale.

I love old photos. I can sit for hours contemplating the people and their lives, making up stories about them.

Nestled in a box of old books, the album beckoned to me. I dusted off the cover and slowly turned the long black pages. Group shots showed young ladies in the Women's Army Auxiliary, wearing wide grins, dress uniforms, and black low quarters, pocketbooks draped across their shoulders.

As I flipped through the pages the photographs seemed to come alive. I could hear their laugher and feel the special camaraderie they shared.

I wondered which of the women owned the album.

I turned a page and came face to face with my answer.

A sepia toned five by seven of a young woman in uniform occupied the center of the page. *Me-1953* scrawled in the margin. Dark, wavy hair framed her heart shaped face. Her eyes sparkled and her smile seemed almost mischievous.

Mesmerized, I felt her pulling me closer and

closer.

"Can I help you?"

Startled, I looked up shading my eyes against the sun.

A woman towered over me.

"I was just looking at the old photos."

She glanced down at the album without comment.

"Who is she?" I asked.

"Lucille Carmichael, my husband's aunt. She served in the Army—in the fifties, I think."

She motioned toward the box of books. "Five dollars for the whole box."

I stood and dug into my pocket. I handed her the money, placed the album on top of the books, and picked up the box.

"Thanks."

I started to leave, then stopped. "Excuse me?"

She turned, her eyebrows arched, alluding to an unspoken question.

"What happened to her? Lucille, I mean."

"Lucille? She taught school for many years. Never married, no children. She lives in a nursing home across town. Why do you ask?"

I shrugged. "Seems a shame she left all these memories behind."

She shook her head.

"She has Alzheimer's. Most days she doesn't even know where she is. She lives in her memories now."

I turned away, saddened by the thought of Lucille, alone in her dementia. I thought about Lucille as I drove home.

Teri met me in the doorway.

"Hey, I'm just leaving. Where have you been all day?"

"Garage saling. I found this great old photo album."

I set the box down and picked up the album.

"Later, okay. I'm meeting Sue and Al and I'm late. As usual."

"Oh, sure. Later."

"Why don't you join us?" she asked. "Dinner at Good Earth? Swing by the Copa later."

"No, thanks. I've got some things I need to do."

She shook her head. "You need to get out and meet people, Kelly. It's been long enough. If you change your mind, come on down. See ya." She bounded down the steps.

I lugged the box into my room and dumped the books on the bed. I placed Lucille's photograph on my bedside table and sat on the bed with the books. Lucille had apparently taught American literature. Most of the books were outdated textbooks and collections of short stories and poetry. Notes filled the margins, her handwriting neat and compact. I shuffled through the pile and came across a dog-eared copy of a book of poetry. The book fell open to a page marked with fading highlighter. I scanned the lines. Rich words touched my heart. I longed for a love so intense, so sensual.

Tears filled my eyes. I studied Lucille's face, and then turned my attention back to the album. The photographs showed Lucille and her fellow G.I. Janes, serving in the Orient, smiling, arm in arm. Again, I heard the noise of the glamorous city streets, the sounds of a moving stream, the laughter of the women. The smell of cherry blossoms filled my room. I traced Lucille's face gently. My eyelids grew heavy. I stretched out on the bed and drifted into a deep sleep. In my dream Lucille invited me to join her.

"Kelly," she called. "I love you. I'm waiting. Come to me."

She reached for me. I felt her hands on my cheeks and the warmth of her lips against mine.

When I awoke I felt confused. "Lucille?"

I sat up and turned on the lamp. The light fell across her face. Her eyes followed me as I moved around the room.

I picked up the photograph.

"Who are you?" I asked. "I feel as though I know you. Am I losing my mind?"

Teri's right. I need to go out. I need to get on with my life. I picked up Lucille's picture and carefully placed it in the album.

I glanced at the clock. Nine-thirty.

I showered, threw on some clothes, and headed for the door. Something called me back. I grabbed the album and left the house. With the album in the back seat I headed for the Copa. It had been months since I'd been out to the bar, afraid of running into my ex and her new lover. Darcy and I had split up nearly a year ago but it still hurt me to think of her with someone else.

I stood in the doorway of the bar. The crowded dance floor pulsated, the bass thumping the floor.

"Kelly!" Teri stood at a table. Sue and Al turned and waved.

I moved toward them.

"Kelly," a familiar voice called.

I stopped and turned, expecting to see an old friend and found myself face to face with Lucille, in full military regalia. She stood an arm's reach from me, more beautiful than her photos had revealed.

The noisy crowd faded. The lights dimmed. All I could see was Lucille.

"Lucille?" I whispered.

"Yes, my love. I'm waiting for you."

I shook my head slowly. "We've never met."

"I'm waiting for you." Her green eyes sparkled. She smiled and my stomach flipped. "We'll be together. Always."

I reached out to touch her and everything went black.

"Kelly? Kelly? Are you alright?"

I opened my eyes.

Teri knelt over me.

"Lucille?" I glanced around but didn't see her.

"Who?" Teri asked.

"The woman who was talking to me, didn't you see her? She was wearing an Army uniform."

"An Army uniform? In here?" she asked. "You must have bumped your head when you fainted." She helped me toward the table.

"You okay, Kelly?" Al asked.

"You look like you saw a ghost," Sue added.

"I think I did," I said.

"Beep, beep, back that truck up," Al said. "You saw a ghost in here? What, some disco-age drag queen?"

"Quit kidding, Al. I think she's serious." Sue placed her hand on top of mine. "What's wrong, Kelly?"

"I think I'm in love with a woman I've never met," I explained. "I'm in love with a photograph."

"Oh jeez," Teri said. "It's that old photo album, isn't it? You ever see Christopher Reeve in that movie where he becomes obsessed with Jane Seymour, named *Somewhere in Time*? Only she's long dead? All it got him was very dead."

"I know, Teri. But you don't understand. She was standing right in front of me."

"You are definitely flesh hungry," Sue said. "You need some loving. Maybe just a good, old-fashioned one-night stand. A little pressing of the flesh and you'll be as good as new."

"That's not it," I said, rubbing my hand over my eyes. "She's real. She called to me. She said she loves me."

They glanced at each other. No one spoke.

"I think I better go home."

"Relax," Al said. "It's only 11:00 p.m. You just got here."

"Uh oh," Sue said.

I followed her eyes toward the door. Darcy and her lover stood in the doorway. My heart fell. Darcy caressed her love with her hands and her eyes. I felt sick.

"It's okay, Kelly. Ignore them."

"I'm not ready for this." I leapt from my seat and ran for the door. I heard Darcy laugh as I pushed past her.

I ran blindly toward my car, my eyes filled with tears, my ears filled with the taunting sound of Darcy's laughter. Fumbling, I started the car and pulled from the parking lot.

I stopped at the light and stared into the rearview mirror. "You look like shit," I said.

Then I saw her. Lucille sat quietly in the back seat of my car. I yanked my head toward the back seat. She wasn't there. The album lay on the seat, open to the photograph of Lucille. I reached for the album and held it close to my chest.

"God, I'm losing my mind," I cried.

The sound of a car horn jolted me. I dropped the album and pulled quickly into the intersection, turning toward home.

"You're not crazy."

I turned sharply. Lucille watched me from the passenger seat. My heartbeat wildly. "Oh god, oh god," I whispered. I couldn't take my eyes off her.

"Watch the road, Kelly," she said softly.

"Are you real?" I asked. My eyes flicked back and forth between the road and Lucille.

"Very real, Kelly," she said as she grinned.

"But, how? You look just like you did in the album. That was what, forty-five years ago?"

"Uh-huh," she said. "The happiest years of my life. I never forgot them. Or you?"

"Me? What are you talking about?"

"Be honest with yourself, Kel. You've always felt out of sync with the rest of the world. Like you've been here before, been through it already? And something's missing."

I listened as she described me to a T. Tears filled my eyes.

"You and I were together. In love and inseparable."

"What happened?" I whispered, afraid of the answer.

"They called you in as part of a witch hunt. Threatened to tell your folks you were a lesbian unless you cooperated. You refused to give up one name. But..." Her voice broke. She turned toward the window.

"Tell me."

"You were ashamed to face your parents. You killed yourself. Jumped from the roof of the dormitory."

"And you?"

"I spent my whole life loving you, Kel. Waiting

for you to return to me. I knew you would someday."

"But how…"

"I died tonight. Just a couple of hours ago." She nodded toward the cell phone. You can call and see for yourself."

I pulled off to the side of the road and reached for the phone.

Lucille placed her hand on top of mine. A tingle ran through me. My breath caught in my throat. Our eyes met. Our lips met.

"Don't leave me, Lucille."

"I can't take you with me," she said. "You have to come on your own. But I'll be waiting for you. All our friends are waiting. We'll be together again. Forever."

And then I was alone.

I sat on the side of the road for a long time. When Teri mentioned *Somewhere in Time*, I know she meant it as a warning. Christopher Reeve's character may have ended up dead but he also found what he had been searching for—eternal love. I didn't have time to will myself into the past. I knew what I had to do.

As the car picked up speed, my thoughts turned to Lucille, our friends, and the Orient.

"Wait for me, Lucille. I'm coming, darling."

As I turned the wheel toward the abutment the smell of cherry blossoms filled the air.

Vickie Adams is a retired military officer. Her short stories have been published in anthologies, including Hot + Bothered, Wilma Loves Betty, Beginnings, Skin Deep, Seducing the Virgin, and UniformsEx, under the pseudonym Lou Hill. Vickie is working on three novels. She lives in Michigan with her partner, three dogs, and nine birds.

Crossroads

By Shannon M. Harris

Ivy stuffed a couple of T-shirts and three pairs of cargo pants into her duffle bag, along with her toiletries and threw it on the bed beside a pair of sneakers and dress shoes.

"Are you sure about this?" Her sister asked.

No, she wasn't sure about anything. She bit her lip and eyed the clothes hanging in her closet. Only the best would do. She ran her fingers along the collar of the blue button-down shirt and remembered the first time they met eight years ago.

Ivy had just gotten off a four-day rotation on Blyter Region's outer moons. As soon as her shuttle docked on Sala, a neutral resting station, Bryan, her mechanic had run off to meet up with his sister, and she had gotten a room, showered, then went in search of something to eat.

The bustle of the station never failed to set her nerves on edge. It might have been neutral ground, but half of these beings, wouldn't blink an eye to attack her once she was out of safe air space. Even though weapons were allowed, you would be permanently banned if you were caught using one. No matter, she still felt a sense of comfort from the phaser strapped around her leg. Her father had gifted it to her when she was fourteen, six years ago.

She ignored the stares as she entered the establishment and nodded her thanks when she was seated in a booth toward the back of the room, away from prying eyes. Once the waitress took her order, she pulled out her tablet and looked over her calendar, purposely keeping her gaze averted from the group that had just entered.

The Penkos were officially known as traders, but everyone knew their practices were unscrupulous in the best of times. They were thieves and had no honor. In the war of the Triads, their kind had used underhanded tactics to kill hundreds of thousands of innocents. It wouldn't bother her one bit if their entire planet was wiped out.

She looked up when they started hollering, clapping, and stomping their feet. The five men moved out of the way to allow a woman to pass through. Once she was clear of them, the woman bowed and grinned at them.

"Please, please," she said. "Don't stop on my account." She placed her hands on her chest and laughed.

When the woman turned in her direction, Ivy swallowed as those deep blue eyes settled on her. The signature gray hair of the Penkos, fell in curls around the woman's shoulders and she had the marks of a warrior, two red lines, around two inches long, tattooed on the side of her neck.

Ivy knew what those marks meant. This woman had killed and not just a few but a lot. It was one thing to have one mark, but two was almost unheard of.

Whoever she was, she wasn't some lowly soldier. This woman was high ranking, or royalty.

Disgust coiled in her stomach and she turned from the woman's fiery gaze. If she hadn't been so hungry, she would have left, but the granola bar she ate three hours ago, was long gone. She thanked the waitress when her stew was set on the table, along with several pieces of bread.

"Excuse me?"

Ivy swallowed, set her spoon back in her bowl, and discreetly slid her left hand to the handle of her phaser. She slowly turned her head and caught the Penkos woman's eyes. There were a lot of things she could have said, but she wasn't here for trouble, and she would behave because Bryan didn't deserve them to be banned from the station. "Can I help you?"

Without asking for permission, the Penkos woman slid into the seat across from her, leaned back against the cushion, and laid her arm across the back of the seat.

"Come here often?"

Ivy blinked and glanced around the room, but no one was looking at them. Did she just really ask her that? Did she not know what race she was?

"Who wants to know?"

She held out her hand, and Ivy only hesitated for a moment before lifting her hand from her phaser and clasping the one across from her. Soft fingers caressed her hand before sliding out of her grasp.

"Resha."

"Ivy."

Resha cocked her head. "So, come here often? I only ask because I have a proposition for you."

"Just like that?" Ivy snapped her fingers and ignored her comm beeping in her pocket.

"Why not? You have something I want."

"Look, my shuttle doesn't carry cargo. Do you know what I am?" Ivy said.

"I have eyes. Yes, I know you are an Amdon." Resha shrugged. "Should that concern me? The war's been over for hundreds of years." She narrowed her eyes. "Don't tell me you're still holding a grudge?"

"You have some nerve."

"You have no idea." Resha rested her elbows on the table and leaned forward. "So, about that proposition?"

"I don't have anything of value. I'm not sure what you want."

Resha licked her lips. "You. I want you."

Ivy sucked in a breath and shook her head. Was this really happening? Could this really be happening? That was the last thing she expected.

Resha grasped Ivy's hand across the table. "I stop here every four months. It would be nice to know I have someone waiting for me and I don't have to look for company."

Ivy jerked her hand back. "I am not a body slave."

"I didn't think you were. If I wanted one, I could easily acquire one."

"Why me?"

Resha bit her bottom lip. "I saw you when you arrived. Those leather pants hugged your ass like a glove. You're hot and I want to fuck you. Why not you?"

Ivy swallowed. Why was she even hesitating? She hated Resha's kind. She pulled her comm out when it beeped again. It was Bryan informing her he would be ready at eight in the morning. She slipped it back in her pocket and ate a bit of her stew when the waitress set a steak on the table in front of Resha and a glass of clear liquid. She was pretty sure that wasn't water.

When the table was cleared, Resha dabbed her lips with her napkin. "Are you going to join me in my room?"

Ivy threw a few bills on the table and stood up. "No." The disappointment that flickered on Resha's face only gave her pause for a second.

"You're coming back to my room with me." Ivy said.

She might still hold out some hostile feelings toward Resha's kind, but it had been a while since she'd spent the night with a beautiful woman. One night couldn't hurt.

Resha stood up and followed her out of the restaurant. Ivy kept her back to Resha and nodded at the people that passed them and spit at the few people who dared to make a derogatory comment toward them. When one particular man passed by them and slurred his words, Resha slipped her arm around Ivy's waist, not allowing her to miss her stride.

"They're not worth it," she whispered in Ivy's ear.

Once at her room, Ivy gripped her key, and didn't comment when Resha slipped it from her hand and waved it over the lock. When the click sounded, Ivy pushed the door open and pulled her jacket off while Resha shut the door. Ivy slid her hands in her pockets and took in the woman in front of her.

Alone, Resha didn't look all that intimidating, but there was no mistaking she was powerful and attractive. If it had been any other species she would have been concerned but she knew the Penkos anatomy was the same as hers.

"So…" She rocked back on her heels and stiffened when Resha stepped in front of her, slipped her arms around her waist, and pulled their bodies flush together. Her heart pounded in her chest and she closed her eyes.

Resha smelled sweet, with a touch of spice. Without opening her eyes, she slid her arms around Resha and ran her hands up her back and gripped her shoulders, before rising and biting her ear.

Resha threw her head back and laughed. "Oh, Ivy. I think we're going to have a lot of fun."

Ivy yelped when Resha lifted her up, and wrapped her legs around Resha's waist.

"You might not know this about my species, but we are extremely strong." Resha said.

"Shut up and put those muscles to use," said Ivy.

With the first taste of Resha's lips and the swipe of her tongue, Ivy knew she was a goner. Resha laid her on the bed with ease, and straddled her, keeping her entire weight from pressing down on Ivy.

"You sure about this?" Resha asked.

Instead of answering her, Ivy leaned forward, grabbed Resha's shirt and pulled it over her head. She let her eyes linger on Resha's chest and toned abs, before licking her way from her collarbone up her neck.

Resha shuddered above her. "I'll take that as a yes."

❧❧❧❧

Ivy was jerked from her memories when her sister shook her arm. "You with me now?"

"Yes, and yes I'm sure about this. We meet every four months. This is not going to be any different."

Her sister smiled sadly. "If you say so. Her family's going to be there, aren't they?"

Of course her family would be there. "I'm trying not to think about it."

"You said her brother was sending you a pass for

their landing station." She zipped Ivy's bag for her.

"I received it yesterday." She hugged Elisha tight. "I'll be fine. Don't worry so much."

"I love you. Of course I worry." She sobered. "I've heard their ceremonies are beautiful."

Ivy turned her face away. "That's what I hear."

"Ivy, you don't have to do this." She gripped her forearm. "You really don't. No one would think badly of you if you didn't go."

Ivy sighed. "Yes, I do—If only to say goodbye. I need the closure."

"Well." She took a step back. "I'm just a tap of the comm away."

"I need to get going." Ivy said.

"I'll see you in a few days."

"Fingers crossed." The truth was, the flight plan she had mapped out wouldn't be easy to transverse, but she had a good feeling she wouldn't be attacked on the trip. Over the years, her shuttle had been tied to Resha and her group. She still didn't know whether that was a good or bad thing, but if it granted her safe passage she would take it.

She settled into her shuttle, engaged the flight plan, and only relaxed when she was given the all clear and took flight. After initializing the cruise control, she kicked her feet up and grabbed the bag of dried fruit she packed and thought back to two years ago when they'd meet up at an outpost outside of Sanmoron Region. It wasn't exactly neutral territory, but they were a peaceful people and they both felt comfortable exploring the area. It was the first time since they'd met that she felt like they'd turned a corner and were more than fuck buddies.

A grin split her face when she spied Resha and three of her men haggling with a merchant. Over the years, she'd learned there was more to Resha than what she saw. Besides having a wicked sense of humor, she was mellow, but lacked patience. Gone were her ideals the Penkos were thieves. Resha had set her straight on more than one occasion concerning her people.

She stood back and admired the way her leather pants and short sleeve shirt hugged her curves. The gun on her hip hung low, and she knew where every one of her other weapons were hidden. She'd never tell Resha… she'd been approached by more than one bandit about betraying her. The thought had never crossed her mind, and she made it clear that would never be an option for her. She'd made more than one enemy along the way, but wouldn't change anything.

She licked her lips when Damor, Resha's second in command pointed in her direction and Resha nodded and motioned for her to join them. She'd been shocked the first time Resha had inquired of her opinion dealing with her business. "Resha…Damor."

"Love." Resha slipped her arm around her waist, pulled her close, and kissed her on the cheek. "We're almost finished here, then we can get going."

"Take your time. I'm off the next few days." Ivy kept her mouth shut as they kept negotiating, and breathed a sigh of relief when they finally agreed on a price.

"Sorry." Resha slipped her arms around her back and hugged her tight.

"It's really not a problem. Let's get out of here." Ivy accepted her kiss, but pushed her back, when things got too heated. "There is plenty of time for that later. I believe you promised me a trip to the museum and dinner at the Belvor Eatery."

"You are right, my Lady." She entwined their fingers and tugged her along the cobbled walkway. They'd been through a lot over the last two years, and she suspected that she wasn't the only woman Resha spent her time with, how could she be, but she would take what she could get. The first year, she had strayed a few times, but found that the few times a year she spent with Resha more than made up for what she was offered from other women. Resha and Ivy started sending each other messages every week or so to keep in touch.

They paid their museum entry fee and spent a few hours admiring the hundreds of relics that had been collected over the years. Quite a few people sent them dirty looks, and she heard murmuring about how could Ivy freely be seen with a Penkos. She ignored them and held tighter to Resha's hand and received a blinding smile in return.

Resha lifted their clasped hands and kissed Ivy's knuckles. "I am always honored of the time we spend together. I know it hasn't always been easy, but I wouldn't trade our time together for anything."

"Do you ever wonder how we got here?" Ivy pointed between them.

"Nope." She winked. "I know exactly how we got here." She grinned and squeezed Ivy's hand. "It all started in a booth, in a restaurant, on a station."

That night she held Resha just a little bit tighter as they slept. She would never tell her she loved her, but the words were always there on the tip of her tongue. That weekend, something had shifted in their relationship. It wasn't unwelcome, but it was unexpected...At least for

Ivy. Resha's kiss right before they parted, felt more like a beginning, than a see you later.

❧ ❧ ❧ ❧

Ivy lifted her feet off the console when a beeping sound reached her ears. She shifted out of cruise and landed at the refueling station. There were several shuttles already grounded, and she easily landed next to an empty spot. She nodded and flipped the attendant an extra coin to fill her tanks.

She stocked up on snacks and was just walking out of the station when she was stopped with a hand on her arm. "Damor. What can I do for you?" Ivy said. He was the last person she wanted to talk to.

"How are you doing, Ivy? I know we're not really friends, but I figure you're headed to the ceremony." He stuffed his hands in his pockets.

"I am."

"I…" He ran his fingers through his hair. "I don't know what to say. I never thought it would come to this. Well, I knew it would. I just thought it would be further down the road."

She laughed. "Me either. I guess we all took for granted how freely she moved around. But, if we really considered it, it was only a matter of time." Life could change in the blink of an eye.

He laughed. "I guess."

"Are you going?" She fiddled with the bag in her hand.

"I'll be there. Her mom asked me to speak."

"Better you than me. I'm still not sure her family will welcome me."

He frowned at her. "They will. No worries."

He looked like he wanted to say more, but kept quiet.

"I guess I'll see you there." She gave the attendant another coin, and closed the hatch on her shuttle. She didn't bother to set the cruise, because if her calculations were right, she would reach her destination in less than an hour.

She'd never been to Resha's planet before and easily touched down when she was given the all clear. After securing her shuttle, she grabbed her duffle bag and exited. What she hadn't expected was Resha to be waiting for her.

"Ivy, I never expected to see you on my planet." Her smile was sad, but held promise. "I'm glad you're here."

Ivy swallowed the lump in her throat. "Me too."

"Come." She held out her hand. Ivy didn't hesitate when Resha grasped it and allowed Resha to lead her through the building. After several turns and three rides, on separate elevators they exited into a large living area. "My home," Resha said.

If she hadn't known her for so long, she would have never recognized her. Gone was the worn leather, and beat up vests and weapons. She still wore leather pants, but in pristine condition, with a blue sleeveless cotton top, embroidered, with what Ivy figured was her house of arms. Her long hair was put up in a bun.

Gone was the roguish girl she met all those years ago and in her place, was the leader of the Penkos people. "You look relaxed," Ivy said. She looked more than relaxed, she looked calm and at peace. Ivy's heart broke at the implication of what she was seeing. Their meetings on far off planets were over.

Resha laughed and clapped her hands together.

"I am. I really am. I didn't expect to be in this situation so quickly, but here I am." She spread her arms wide and the gold bracelets on her wrist jingled. The last time she saw her, a leather cuff adorned that wrist.

Ivy gulped and shook off her nerves. This was still her Resha after all—at least for another day or so. Then she would be bonded with another and Ivy would be on her way home, alone.

"I was sorry to hear about your father," Ivy said.

"He passed quickly, with a smile on his face. It's what we all wished for him."

"I guess congratulations are in order." She fidgeted with the hem of her shirt.

Resha nodded, then took a seat on the couch, motioning for Ivy to do the same. "A lot has changed since the last time we saw each other."

"Four months and three days." Ivy would count the days until they got to see each other again.

"We didn't speak often of the customs of my people, but we both knew what would happen. We might have ignored them, but they were always there under the surface. We both know I cannot be crowned the leader of my people without first taking a spouse. Someone I can lean on, share my joys and fears with— someone to help me lead my people. Someone I can raise a family with."

She was right, they hadn't talked much about what Resha's life would be like and the one time they had talked about it, Ivy didn't want to listen or hear what she was saying. Now she wished she would have taken her more seriously. The Penkos ways were not the same as hers. Maybe it would have stopped her heart from breaking.

❧ ❧ ❧ ❧

Their third meeting in their fourth year found them both cuddled up on the couch in Resha's suite. Ivy was content to lay in the silence, but Resha had seemed like she had something on her mind all evening and if the way she was squirming on the couch was any indication, she was about to share what was bothering her.

"Ivy, I know we usually steer clear of talking about our home worlds, but I think it's time we talked about what my people's customs are like and what that means for me. For us."

"All right." Ivy lifted Resha's hand and started playing with her fingers. "I'm listening."

The truth was she didn't want to know. It would feel like an invasion into the bubble they had created for themselves, but she wouldn't deny Resha anything. Not if it was within her power.

"As you well know, I will one day take my father's place and lead my people."

She did know. It hadn't come as any surprise that Resha's father was the sovereign of the Penkos. "I do."

Resha sighed and held onto Ivy a bit tighter. "I fear that day will come quicker than either one of us expect. He's been quite sick this year. Mother thinks he only has a few years left. It's the custom of my people that I cannot take over his position without first having a spouse. It is written that the leader needs a partner to keep them balanced."

Ivy closed her eyes. "Why are you telling me this now?"

"You need to know when the time comes, I will have no choice but to take a wife. I might enjoy the roaming life now, but when the time comes, it will be

an honor to take over my father's position. I'm ready."

"Are you breaking up with me?" She cringed at the crack in her voice. When this started between them, the last thing she expected were feelings to develop.

"No." She turned Ivy around to sit on her lap. Ivy straddled her and wrapped her arms around her neck and Resha rested her hands on her hips. "No. We will just have to be prepared when the time comes."

They sat in silence until Ivy asked the question that was at the forefront of her mind. "Will she be a stranger or someone you know?"

"Someone I know. My family will make sure to make an informed choice."

Ivy pulled back. "You don't get to pick?"

She shook her head. "No. They will pick for me."

"You're okay with that?" That seemed out of character for her.

"I am. My family loves me and I know they only want what's best for me." She tucked a loose strand of hair behind Ivy's ear.

"Can't you marry beforehand?"

"I can, but to make the ceremony binding it would have to be done on my home planet with my family in attendance."

"I see." She nuzzled Resha's neck. She was comfortable with Resha but she wasn't sure how she would deal with an entire planet of her people. She didn't want to think about this. Not now. "I don't know about you, but I've missed our time together." She licked her lips.

"Ivy, are you okay?"

"I will be."

Resha didn't look convinced, but Ivy silenced her with a kiss.

"We only have two days. Let's make the most of them."

"There isn't anywhere else I would rather be." And Ivy believed her.

⚜⚜⚜⚜

Ivy shook her head. "I know you have to take a partner and I also know I don't have any reason to be jealous, but…"

Resha cut her off. "On the contrary, I think you have every reason to be jealous. I would be if our roles were reversed. If we hadn't been from two different worlds I would have asked you to bond with me years ago."

Ivy ran her hands down her pants. "I would have said no."

Resha scooted forward on the couch. "That's why I never asked. We were both in two different places. Now, I don't have a choice but to bond with someone." Her eyes were pleading with her to understand.

"I know, Resha. I know." Ivy stood up and started pacing. "I needed to see you one last time. Clear the air. Get some closure." She threw her hands in the air and turned toward Resha. "Does that make sense? My sister was trying to get me to stay away." She laughed. "Where did the time go?" Ivy said.

"Do you know?" Resha stood up and slipped her arms around Ivy's waist and pulled until she was settled back against her chest. "That since our first meeting, you captured my heart. I saw you sitting there with a scowl on your face, and I had to talk to you. There was this pull. I couldn't deny it and I was hoping you wouldn't be able to either."

Ivy melted into her embrace and closed her eyes, just enjoying being with her.

Resha continued with Ivy's silence. "After our first meeting, I told my parents about you. They were happy, but also told me to be cautious. You would break my heart, they said, but I continued to see you anyway."

"Why?" She sniffled and wiped her eyes.

"Like I said. You captured my heart."

Ivy swallowed. "Do you love her?"

"Ivy?"

"Do you love her?" Ivy said a bit more forcefully then she had intended to when Resha stiffened behind her.

"Ivy you should know by now that I couldn't possibly love another." Resha tried to move away, but Ivy tightened her hands on the arms wrapped around her.

"If you ask me to bond with you, I will say yes." Ivy said.

"How can I ask you to stay, knowing what a wanderer you are? You love to roam freely. Here you will have obligations and commitments. You will live out the rest of your life in a strange environment. One you may never be comfortable in." She rested her chin on Ivy's shoulder.

"But, I'll have you," Ivy said quietly.

"I can't take your freedom from you."

"I'm giving it freely." She hadn't told her sister, but she had a feeling she already knew. She'd always intended to stay if Resha asked her to. She loved her, after all. They'd always been moving toward this point in time. It just took a little longer for them to get here.

Resha spun her around.

"Ivy, since I first laid eyes on you, you have been the only woman in my life."

Ivy's eyes widened. "What?"

"I know there have been others for you, but for me, you've always been the one. I might not have always showed it, but I hope you always knew I cared. Far more in the beginning then I should have."

Ivy closed her eyes and laid her head on Resha's chest and said, "After the first six months, you've been the only one for me."

The arms around Ivy tightened. "What a pair we make. Who would have expected two women from completely different backgrounds and worlds to come together? What's it been? Eight years? I do believe our bond will be the first of its kind on my planet." She chuckled.

Ivy pulled back and was sure the grin on her face was as big as the one on Resha's.

"Well, you haven't asked me yet and doesn't your family have to approve of me first?"

That was her one fear. After everything, Resha's family wouldn't approve of her.

"Oh, Ivy. You were my family's only choice. They knew I would never be satisfied with anyone but you. You don't have anything to worry about. My family is happy for me. You may still have your reservations about my people, but they don't have any about you."

Resha moved away from her, walked across the room, and picked up a bracelet that was lying on top of the dresser. Instead of waiting for Resha to walk back, Ivy went to her. Resha picked up Ivy's hand and laid the bracelet over her wrist, but didn't clasp it.

"Ivy, would you do the honor of bonding with me?"

"Yes."

Resha secured the bracelet, then lifted Ivy up off the floor and swung her around, peppering her face with kisses.

"I love you."

"Oh, Resha, I love you too."

"Did you always intend to stay?"

"Did you always intend to ask?"

Resha kissed her on the cheek.

"When my father died, I was at a crossroads. One way would lead me to you and the other would lead to my new life. I didn't think I could have both, but when I was young my father told me something that has stuck with me."

"What's that?" Ivy pulled back enough to look into Resha's eyes.

"He told me that if I was ever at a crossroads and couldn't decide on which path I should take, I should start walking a new one and that's exactly what I'm doing. Will it be easy for us, I hope so, but there will always be obstacles in the way. I'm confident that together, we can overcome anything thrown in our path."

Ivy squeezed her tight, content to just be with her. This wasn't what she expected for herself at all, but the woman in her arms was the future she wanted. When they first met all those years ago, she would have laughed it off if someone would of told her this would be her future.

"I think it's time I met your family." Ivy said.

"In a moment."

Resha lowered her head and kissed her. It took all of Ivy's strength not to melt on the spot.

Ivy grinned and said. "There is never going to be

a dull moment with you,"

Yes, this was exactly where she wanted to be.

"Oh, Ivy, you have no idea. I may be the leader of my people, but I'm still a badass." She tapped her on the nose. "And don't you forget it."

Shannon M. Harris is the author of four published novels and two short stories with Sapphire Books. She lives in Southern Illinois with her three cats Lillie, Charlie, and Shady McQuinn. In her spare time she enjoys reading, listening to music, and binge watching the I.D. channel.

The New Muse

By T.L. Hayes

The writer sat down at her desk, cup of coffee on the left side of her keyboard, in the one uncluttered spot left for that purpose. She opened a new document on her computer and stared at the stark whiteness in front of her. She knew what this book was going to be about. It was already plotted, with characters that already had rich backstories. It was going to be awesome, it was going to be her best yet, but it wasn't going to be anything if she couldn't write the first word. She sat back in her chair and sighed. She had to do it. Her proposal had been accepted and she now had a deadline and a big check waiting for her when she did. That was enough to galvanize her and she sat forward and put her hands back on the keyboard. She got two words written and her cell phone vibrated next to her on the desk. Unable to ignore it, she picked it up and saw that she had a message from that woman from the dating site, the one with the sexy voice she had yet to meet. She smiled. She unlocked her phone and pulled up the message.

The New Muse: "Busy?"

Writer: "Yes, writing."

The New Muse: "Hmm, such a turn on."

"Really? Wow. Okay, I can work with this."

Realizing she was talking to an empty room, the writer went back to her phone.

Writer: "If that turns you on, you should let me read you some of my short stories. I think you'll like them."

The New Muse: "Writing does turn me on. Mmm, would you read it to me? Yes, that is definitely something we should make happen."

Writer: "Yes, but sadly not now. I have a deadline and I need to get started."

The New Muse: "But don't I inspire you? Show me."

The writer groaned and thought. *Oh god, does she have any idea? Oh, I'm sure she does.*

Writer: "Yes you do but I'm trying to write a novel about suicide and this is not getting me in the right frame of mind. But later, I promise..."

The New Muse: "Okay, go write. But you will read to me sooner or later."

Writer: "I promise."

The writer put her phone back down and approached her keyboard again, and attempted to write for a second time. She was attempting to write a serious novel for the first time, one based on personal experience. It would be touching and sad and have all the feels. It would probably make her cry. She hoped it touched people.

Don't I inspire you? Said the new muse. "Get out of my head!" The writer said out loud. *Show me.* "Not now!" Said the writer. *Read to me. Touch me. The new muse baited.* "She never said that, stop it!" The writer shouted.

But, it was too late. The old muse the writer was wrestling with was gone. A new one was taking hold.

The writer sighed. She leaned back in her chair, closed her eyes and said, "What do you want to show me?"

The writer knocked on the new muse's door. When the muse answered it, she wore a smirk but didn't seem surprised at the writer's sudden appearance on her doorstep. She just leaned against her doorframe and crossed her arms over her chest. "Yes?"

"You've been teasing me."

The muse chuckled evilly. "I have. What are you going to do about it?"

The writer said nothing, she just stepped forward and put her hands on the muse's waist, linking her fingers into the belt loops of the muse's jeans and pulled her close. The muse came willingly, now laughing, as she put her arms around the writer's neck, kissing the writer before she could make the move to do so. Just as their tongues started to find each other, the muse pulled back from the kiss, the smirk turning into a smile.

"No more teasing." The writer pulled the muse to her more roughly this time and started walking forward and pushing the muse inside the house as she did so. She kicked the door closed behind her as she leaned in for another kiss. This time her hands rapidly pulling at the blue T-shirt the muse was wearing while the muse was clawing at hers. The writer put her hands under the shirt, feeling the hot flesh beneath, running her hands across the belly and along the sides, letting her fingers slip below the waistband of the muse's jeans, grabbing her hips.

The muse had her arms around the writer's neck but at the feel of the hands on her hips, she thrust forward and moaned, pushing more of herself against the writer, breast to breast and she pulled back just far enough to grab the writer's bottom lip with her teeth, sucking it into her mouth and holding it hostage. The writer moaned and the muse let out a throaty chuckle as she released her. "You mean I can't tease you just a little bit?"

"Oh, I think you can tease me a lot. But, as I said, *no more teasing.*" Just as the writer lunged forward to attack the muse's neck, her phone buzzed again.

"Goddammit!" She leaned forward in her chair and grabbed her phone, hoping it was another text from her new muse so she could keep the fantasy going, but it wasn't.

Best Friend: "How's the writing coming?"

It was her best friend, a fellow writer working on her own projects. She didn't approve of the new muse and the writer had a wild thought that she knew where her current thoughts had been going and was trying to derail them on purpose. Her friend could be spooky like that when she wanted to be.

Writer: "Okay. Was taking a break."

Best Friend: "Well, good luck with it. I'm here if you need me."

That was the problem, she was there too, in the writer's head, and she had no business being there. But, it was too late, the mood was broken and she couldn't find her way back into the fantasy. "Dammit to hell!" The writer threw her phone back on her desk and approached her keyboard again and started her novel.

❧ ❧ ❧ ❧

It had been days since she'd heard from her new muse, which was good, and bad. It meant the writer got a lot of work done, but in the back of her mind there was still lingering thoughts of the new muse, thoughts of what she could be doing and why she hadn't texted or called. Those had been the only thoughts she allowed, as the other thoughts were too distracting, even if, or maybe more so because they were such delicious thoughts. Whenever they would come, the writer would hastily shoo them away as if they would bite her. Luckily, at least where her deadline was concerned, they always left so that her old muse could do her job. The writer told herself that being productive and staying focused on the bottom line was the best course of action at the moment.

Plus, her best friend, the other writer, the one she called her unofficial life coach because she always gave the best advice, which the writer almost always took, had said via text, "She's not allowed to flirt with you if she doesn't want a relationship." Which is, what the muse had said early on and the writer hadn't challenged it and was okay with it. Then the flirting started and the writer was okay with that too. It didn't have to mean anything other than fun. The writer knew this. Her best friend was a bit overprotective, but not without reason. The best friend had been there when the writer's last relationship had ended and knew what that had done to her. The writer knew she had her best interests in mind but the writer also knew that there was nothing wrong with a little flirting. It was good for the soul and it was damn fun. It was distracting. That didn't mean the writer wouldn't welcome it if it happened again, as she hoped it would.

Just as she was getting to a particularly harrowing part in the novel, finally, the long awaited text came, the one she kept telling herself she hadn't been waiting for. She eagerly stopped typing and picked up her phone and read the message with a smile.

44

The New Muse: "I'm still waiting on you to read to me."

Writer: "Maybe I can read you a bedtime story tonight. How about I call you in a few hours? I have something in mind."

The New Muse: "Sounds wonderful. I hope you'll be in good voice tonight."

Writer: "Baby, my mouth is always in good form. Oral...presentations are my specialty."

The New Muse: "I'll bet. I can't wait. Later."

The writer chuckled to herself, as she pushed the new muse onto the couch, who sat back with a smile on her lips. There was challenge in the muse's eyes. She said, "You got me where you want me. Now what?"

The writer straddled the new muse's lap and reached for the bottom of the muse's T-shirt. The new muse smiled knowingly and raised her arms above her head. The writer pulled the shirt off and threw it aside, revealing that the muse was wearing nothing underneath. She lightly brushed her thumbs over the muse's nipples, pinching the left one, which made the muse moan. Then the writer leaned down and put her mouth on the right nipple, grazing her teeth across it and applying just a bit of pressure. The muse put her arms around the writer and found purchase in the writer's hair, grabbing it with both hands. The writer pressed her teeth down some more, applying enough pressure for a soft bite. This made the muse inhale suddenly and tighten her grip on the writer's hair. The muse started to breathe heavily and the writer intensified her work. She began to suck the nipple into her mouth, while her fingers pinched the left nipple even harder. The muse began to move beneath her and her breathing came in gulps.

"More. I want more." The muse grabbed the writer's right hand and put it in her crotch, pressing her hand on top of it, pushing the writer's hand onto her more. The writer responded by rubbing the muse's crotch through her jeans, making sure to put pressure on the seam in the middle. The muse took her hand off the writer's and grabbed the writer's collar and leaned forward and began to nuzzle the writer's ear. This made the writer moan as well and their voices rose in unison. The muse slowly ran her tongue along the outer edge of the writer's ear, then darted it in for a moment, while the writer quickened her pace with the muse's nipple and rubbing her crotch.

The muse pulled away from the writer's ear and managed to ask, "Don't you want to take off your shirt so I can touch you better?"

Before the writer could respond, her phone buzzed in her pocket. She groaned and pulled it out and opened the message.

Best Friend: "Hope all is going well. I've wanted to say this. I know you like her but I think you need to be careful with her. Don't let her become a muse."

Writer: "Too late, my friend. I know what I'm doing. I wish you trusted me."

Best friend: "Oh, sweetheart, I do trust you. I just want you to guard your heart. I don't want you getting hurt again."

Writer: "Sweetheart? That's new. Thank you but it's okay, really. I was just busy on my novel and she's not the muse for that, so no worries."

Best Friend: "Okay. I know I'm overprotective, but I love you and want the best for you."

"She sounds jealous. I think she's in love with you." The muse said.

The muse now sat with her arms crossed over her chest, shirt back on. The writer sat beside her on the couch.

"No, that's not it, She's just concerned for me. She cares. As she said, she doesn't want me getting hurt. Like any good friend."

The writer reached over and ran her fingers through the muse's long reddish blond hair. The muse smacked her hand away.

"Don't touch my hair," the muse said. Feeling wounded, the writer withdrew her hand.

"Sorry. But, I swear, it's not what you think. She knows all the bad stuff that went on with my ex is all. She's just playing watchdog. I'm glad she's on my side."

The muse snorted. "She doesn't trust me, even though she doesn't know me. Plus, she thinks you can't look out for yourself. What, does she think I'm an evil temptress leading you astray?" The muse smiled wickedly at the writer and reached over and lightly caressed the writer's face with her fingertip.

The writer smiled and ran her fingertips down the muse's arm, causing the muse to shudder and goose bumps to form on her arm. "Yes, she thinks exactly that. You mean you're not?"

"I never said I wasn't, just that she has no way of knowing that about me."

"She just kinda knows things sometimes."

"You mean she's psychic?"

"Something like that or just a really good guesser who knows how to read people. Either way, I end up telling her everything because she's going to figure it out eventually anyway."

"Maybe the feeling between you is mutual. I think you need to figure that out. Until you do, you don't need

me." The muse got up from the couch and walked out of the room.

The writer sat forward in her chair. "Goddammit! So much dyke drama even in my own fantasies."

❧❧❧❧

"So, what did you want to talk about?" The best friend sat facing the writer, with one arm propped on the back of the couch, one leg crossed under her, and a cup of coffee resting on her leg, with the middle fingers of her right hand through the handle. She gave the writer a kind smile. Everything about her was kind, the writer felt, that's partly why they had become so close. She had such a big heart and when you were loved and cared for by her it just made one feel peaceful and glad that she was there for you. But, the writer also knew that her life coach could also be a fierce badass when taking on the enemy and the enemy was anyone who went after the underdog on her watch. The writer admired badassery a great deal.

The writer, with her own coffee in hand, sat in much the same way, facing her friend. "Yeah, just something I kinda need to ask you. Something I've been wondering about." The writer looked down at her cup. She couldn't look at the warmth in her friend's eyes. It was too much.

Her friend put her hand on the writer's knee. "It's okay, whatever it is, you can always talk to me. I hope you know that."

The writer smiled and put her hand over the hand on her knee and entwined their fingers together. Her friend let her do this and scooted a little closer. Finally, she looked back up at her friend. "I was just wondering, I mean, this is probably not even, I mean..." She stopped talking and sighed. "I'm sorry, I don't know how to say this."

The best friend gently let go of the writer's hand, leaned forward and put her cup on the coffee table, then took the writer's from her and placed their cups next to each other. Then she turned back to the writer and took both of her hands in hers.

"It's okay, you don't have to be nervous with me. You have already shared so much with me. Whatever this is, it won't be any different. Now come on, say it."

The writer took a deep breath still holding her friend's hands.

"Okay, I was just wondering if there was something more between us than friendship."

The friend looked confused for a moment, then she gently caressed the writer's cheek with the back of her hand.

"Of course there is. I love you very much."

"You, you do?"

"Of course, I've told you that. This isn't news. We're friends, friends are supposed to love each other."

"Well, yeah, but, but, that's not what I meant."

The friend was silent for a moment, then understanding crossed her face and she let go of the writer's hands. The writer looked down forlornly at their now separated hands, then back up at her friend in confusion. Her friend leaned back and put one arm on the back of the couch again and leaned her head against it and sighed.

"I thought we already had this conversation?" The friend said.

They had. When they had first met, the writer had liked her immediately. Everything about her was perfect in the writer's estimation. She had made her intentions known right off but the woman who would become her best friend had rebuffed her, saying that the writer wasn't her type, and that she had her reasons. Crestfallen, the writer had understood and backed off, having gotten used to rejection. What had followed was the strongest relationship she had ever had with any friend since college. It became a relationship she treasured. And somewhere along the way, the writer stopped thinking of her as a romantic possibility and let the relationship become the friendship it was meant to be.

"I'm sorry, I've just been confused lately. I mean, your reaction to the new, I ah mean, to that woman I like, it's just made me wonder if...if something had changed between us."

The kindness was back in her best friend's eyes when she reached for the writer's hand again. She said, "I see what this is about. I have been acting a little like a jealous girlfriend, haven't I?" She smiled.

"Maybe just a tad." The writer returned her smile.

"I'm sorry, it's just that...it's just that...it's just that I want to protect you. I want to keep you from women like your ex and this new one...I worry about her intentions. That's all."

"You mean, you wonder if she just wants to use me for sex?"

"Well, yes."

"Have you considered that that possibility has occurred to me and that I have no problems with that outcome?" She raised an eyebrow at her friend and the friend returned the gesture and her smile grew.

"No, I haven't."

"I'm not a little kid. I can read people too and

am pretty good at seeing their intentions and motives. And I'm an adult who also wouldn't mind getting laid every now and again. And since you're apparently not offering, I have to look elsewhere." The best friend laughed out loud. "I will be fine. Okay?"

The friend laughed at herself. "Okay, okay. And I'm sorry if sometimes my overprotectiveness comes out like I think you're a child, because I don't. I just love you and want the best for you."

"I know that." The writer gave her friend a sly smile. "But you'll totally kick her ass if necessary though, won't you?"

"In a fucking heartbeat." Her friend picked up her coffee cup and drank from it nonchalantly, as if she hadn't just threatened a total stranger.

"Good." The writer picked up her cup as well and held it aloft and they touched mugs and grinned.

Seriously, that's it? Even in my fantasy, all we do is hold hands? Are you fucking kidding me? But, that's good news I guess. Yes! I'm not in love with my best friend. And she's not in love with me because she would totally say all of that. Ha!

❧ ❧ ❧ ❧

The writer leaned forward in her chair, put her hand on her computer mouse and navigated to the open window for the dating site where she had met her new muse, which they no longer needed to communicate through since they had exchanged numbers. She pulled up the pictures the muse had posted and pulled up her favorite one. The muse was standing in a bathtub of all places, fully clothed in jeans and T-shirt, one arm upraised with hand in a victorious fist, the other holding her phone and a look of exalted triumph on her face. The writer liked it because in it the muse showed a lot of her personality, an exuberance with life that was very attractive. The writer wasn't sure if that was what made it seem sexy to her or if it was the muse herself, but either way, the picture worked. *I have to fucking get to Michigan. But first things first, I owe you a bedtime story.* Chuckling to herself, she picked up her phone, leaned back in her chair, and hit the muse's number from her contacts list and waited for the phone to be answered.

When the muse answered she said, "Hello. Is this the bedtime story I ordered?"

"It is. Are you in bed, all snuggled up?"

"Very much so. All alone, waiting for someone to come and tuck me in."

"I'm here to help. I'll do whatever I can to make you comfortable."

"You will?"

"Yes."

"What will you do first?"

The writer smiled and turned away from the short story on her computer screen that she had been prepared to read. It was a short erotic piece about sex in the moment with a stranger, but she quickly realized that she didn't need it. "I would lay you gently back on the bed..."

"Not so gently."

"Alright. I would push you firmly to the bed, my hands on your shoulders then I would lay down on top of you, covering your body with mine. And put a kiss on your lips that would be the promise of what was to come. Our nipples would press together as my hands explored your body and my lips and my tongue exploring your mouth. Your hand would come up to touch my hair but I grab your wrist and hold it down against the mattress, not allowing you to touch me. My lips move from your mouth to your neck, the hollow space between your shoulder and collar bone, and I kiss you there, first gently, then sucking your flesh and grazing your skin with my teeth, until I know I've left my mark. You squirm under me and moan. Your wrist struggling under my hand, wanting to move but can't. Your other hand you use to grab my nipple but, though it feels good, I take the wrist in my other hand and hold it against the mattress as well. I come back up to whisper in your ear. This is about you. Enjoy it. You relax some under me but you move your body against me and I put my lips to your chest and kiss my way to your nipple, again I graze my teeth over your skin and then I gently, at first, bite down on your nipple, causing you to gasp and thrust your hips towards me. I chuckle evilly and bite harder and you cry out."

"Yes! More."

"Yes. I nibble more, then suck hard, bringing your nipple up to its full glory. Once it's erect, I flick my tongue over it, keeping it there, then put my teeth on it again and bite harder than I did last time. I know it's a pleasure pain for you and your moans get loader and your hips thrust fast against me and you strain against my hands holding your wrists. I tighten my grip on your wrists and begin to kiss across and down your body, licking and sucking and nibbling my way down, until my lips find yours. At the same time, I let go of your wrists and grip your fingers in mine, as my tongue darts out and flicks the tip of your clit."

"Oh yes."

"My tongue plays with your clit for several

moments, then I suck it into my mouth, just as I did your nipple, lightly grazing it across my teeth. You buck against me and grip my fingers tightly. My tongue leaves your clit and moves on to the outer lips of your pussy, making its way to the opening, then I curl my tongue so that it can enter you and dart it in and out in a rapid way. I let go of your hands and grab your hips and you entwine your fingers in my hair, holding on."

"Damn, you're good at this."

"Then, I take one hand off your hip and run my fingers around your wetness, moving my tongue up to play with your clit some more, then ease two fingers in."

"More!"

"I slide in a third and pick up speed. I remove my tongue but replace it with my thumb, rubbing your clit, the motion of my wrist as my fingers move in your pussy propelling my thumb faster over your clit."

"Don't stop!"

"While my hand moves within you, I climb up and place a kiss on your lips, your tongue playing with mine, as your fingers claw into my back. As the orgasm hits you, your fingers sink into my flesh and you moan and your whole body shakes. You bite my bottom lip and it almost hurts but I keep going. I pull my lips away but your hands stay on my shoulders and I flip my wrist gently while it's inside you and my fingers beg you to come. I piston my arm faster and faster and you scream out..."

"Oh god!"

"Yes! And I slow my motion gradually, as your body continues to react. As I ease my fingers out, your body shakes and I pull the sheet up over us and place a kiss on your lips and hold you to me and you put your hand on my chest and snuggle into me, your body spent but sated." The writer let out a breath, almost as exhausted as she'd have been if she had actually been doing those things.

The muse was quiet a moment. Then, "Oh my god. That was intense. You sure know how to tell a story."

The writer chuckled evilly. "Thank you. But I'm much better in person."

The muse chuckled as well. "Really? Prove it."

"Are you saying what I think you're saying?"

"I am. I'll be waiting."

After she hung up, after tucking the muse into bed, she sent her best friend a message.

Writer: "I have to follow my new muse. I hope you understand."

Best Friend: "I knew you would. I love you. Be safe."

Writer: "But you will always be my first muse."

Best Friend: "I know that too."

Writer: "Of course you do." The writer smiled to herself as she went back to her computer and booked a flight to Michigan.

Ms. Hayes currently has a novel published through Bold Strokes Books, entitled, A Class Act, and has a second novel coming out through them in August entitled, Sweet Boy and Wild One. She lives in Springfield, IL with four cats and a roommate.

If the Time is Right, Do it Over Skype

By Lisa Blush

Don't be shy. Come on, tell me...please?" Cybil smiled, fully engaged in this budding conversation as she rolled over in bed onto her stomach, and repositioned the phone closer to her ear. She heard a low toned shudder filter down the line and taper off into silence. She asked in a softly prodding tone.

"What are you afraid of?"

She could hear a steady inhale and exhale, but had no idea what was running through Wren's mind. Cybil's mood dropped incrementally from the unpromising silence, and she bit her lip before trying again. She nudged Wren in a desperate whisper.

"It's just me."

She suddenly felt nervous about this, and that was a total mood killer. The longer she had to convince her girlfriend to open up, the more her nerves began to grow until her body tingled with unshed emotion of the unsexy variety.

"I'm embarrassed. It's too much." Wren spoke for the first time in at least two full minutes since Cybil had asked her to share her hottest fantasy. "I don't really know how to talk sexy, I'm sorry, Cybil."

Cybil rolled around in bed again, this time slumping heavily onto her back. She squeezed her eyes closed and pinched the bridge of her nose in a familiar gesture of annoyance.

"We're so good at this when you're here…just be yourself, be like that."

"I can't. It's different when we're just talking and not touching. I express myself better in person," Wren said defensively.

Cybil sensed that she should stop pushing, but she felt lonely and wanted to capture that comforting sense of intimacy. Wren had been away for too long.

"But you're a reporter, expressing yourself through words is what you excel at. Are you feeling the same way that I'm feeling?" Cybil's voice raised just enough to sound like an admonishment, and she instantly regretted it. She recognized that she was calling out her girlfriend for making excuses, but she knew that no matter what words they exchanged over the phone it was a paltry substitute for being together physically.

"I miss you," Wren sighed, her words rushed out in a sad whoosh of utter longing, and then she went quiet again.

Cybil supported Wren's dream of working as an international reporter, and before it became a reality and Wren was sent off to cover news in Europe—far away from home in Chicago—it had seemed like an exotic and fun promotion. After long weeks spent apart, both women were on edge, and Cybil privately wondered if the couple was going to survive this.

She licked her dry lips as she tried to come up with a different tactic to get Wren's mind off the circumstances and back to addressing the nagging ache of sexual neglect that had begun to grow and expand deep in her belly.

"I miss you too. You have no idea," Cybil drew in a sharp breath at the realization of how true that statement was.

She missed their morning routine of waking up together knowing the feeling of safety and warmth. She missed cuddling unguarded like they were the only two people in existence. Things used to be cozy in the early morning. Now Cybil woke without joy and in search of coffee instead of luxuriating with her love, before facing the workday.

The weekends were the worst. Cybil loved making Wren pancakes with fresh strawberries and gobs of whipped cream on Saturday mornings. Her girlfriend had a hearty appetite, but without her around to share meals with, Cybil found that her own eating patterns had become erratic. She often forgot to make dinner or didn't eat until the pain of her empty stomach reminded her. She was lucky to cram down some dry toast in the morning.

"Ask me again," Wren's voice punctuated the silence and broke Cybil from her train of thought.

She frowned in dismay. Whatever feeling had prompted her desire to start this conversation had dissipated. Cybil just wanted to go to sleep and check another day off the calendar page.

"Seriously, I want to try," Wren stated again, whining now, and though the mood had been wholly interrupted Cybil appreciated Wren's resolve, but it was no use. She set about trying to humor her earnest girlfriend anyway.

"Okay, let's start over," Cybil nodded and immediately felt foolish with no one to see her.

She lifted her knees and reached down to pull the covers over her body, settling in on her side of the bed. She looked at the flat undisturbed side designated to Wren, and wished that she would magically appear, preferably naked. She asked the question again at Wren's insistence.

"What's your hottest fantasy?"

Wren answered with a question of her own, "Are you in bed?"

"Yes," Cybil shifted her hips, settling down deeper and sinking into the mattress. She dragged her palm slowly over the sheets focusing on the soft texture. "I'm in our bed thinking of how lovely it would be if you were here too."

"Unfortunately, it's early here," Wren advised with a yawn. "I have to get more minutes for my phone especially if you plan to waste them on this pointless conversation."

Wren had difficulty operating from a place of raw emotion, but that was what Cybil needed. She lamented that it was much easier to nudge Wren when she had the ability to use her tongue for more than speaking.

"I love you, but can you focus on the phone sex before you run out of minutes?"

"Yeah," Wren chuckled, "Sorry, I'm so bad at this. I know you're having a hard time and so am I. I'm not comfortable, like I'm sitting at my desk looking at boring research and thinking about breakfast, not sex. Honestly, my hottest fantasy right now would be to land an on camera interview with this top-level social activist dude."

Cybil ignored her, she knew she was trying to get off topic and let the elephant in the room linger. She pressed on.

"Wren, have you ever wanted to try something

different in bed, but you were afraid that I wouldn't want to try it to?"

She hinted that she knew her girlfriend's preferences well enough to know that there had to be something she wanted to try. She'd seen her face twisted in a vague look of conflicted guilt at times during their lovemaking, like she wanted to ask for something, but all attempts to extract Wren's carefully concealed desires had been shut down.

"Um…why are you asking me that?" Wren was hesitant and sounded snotty.

Cybil gritted her teeth and she attempted to hold her tongue as anger started to rise within her. Her face felt hot and itchy, they were getting nowhere. This sort of head against the wall bashing frustration combined with a one-two punch of horny and lonely feelings was enough to make her lose her patience. This was it. She was just going to be direct.

"What is it? Do you ever want me to spank your bare ass until you're red and squirming in pain? Pull your hair and scratch my nails across your scalp? Maybe you fantasize about having your wrists and ankles bound, and being teased mercilessly while incapacitated? Would you prefer I use a feather or my teeth?"

Cybil started spit balling questions. She really thought Wren would respond positively. She was wrong.

"Shut up! Really? You think I want that?"

Now Wren was pissed off and crying. So much for thinking she would open up.

"When have I ever given you any indication I would enjoy anything remotely like that?"

"I didn't mean to upset you. I thought it would

be easier to talk about this kind of stuff over the phone since you're not here. We've been living together for six months and you won't so much as let me stick a finger up your butt—not even my little pinky!"

"Because I don't like it—I don't like toys or fingers up my butt, and I don't understand why you're hell bent on this topic? Do you—do you want to sleep with someone else while I'm gone? Is that it?" Her voice broke roughly as she yelled at Cybil.

In exasperation, she replied, "No, Wren, of course not."

Cybil felt tears leaking out of her eyes, as horrible feelings of insecurity gnawed at her insides.

"Are you seeing someone else over there?" Unbidden visuals of olive skinned, raven haired, sensuous European women in various sexual positions with her girlfriend flooded her mind.

"I think we should end this conversation now," Wren announced firmly, and Cybil nodded in agreement, stumbling to make a noise of affirmation. "Let's talk about this later. I'm out of minutes anyway." The line went dead.

Cybil dropped her phone onto the pillow and turned onto her side. She pulled her knees up against her chest and let herself go numb. She didn't get much sleep, if any, and when her alarm sounded sharply punctuating the stillness and quiet of her bedroom she started out her day feeling exhausted and heartbroken.

☙ ☙ ❧ ❧

"Hey, *Good Wife*, why are you looking so grumpy?"

Cybil was greeted at the office by her well-meaning paralegal. She narrowed her eyes as she stomped into her office in her high heels and shot Gloria a look of annoyance. Gloria thought it was so funny to refer to Cybil as *The Good Wife* and although she bore a slight resemblance to Juliana Margulies and both Cybil and the fictional character were lawyers who lived and practiced in Chicago, the similarities ended there.

"Can you stop calling me that, please?" Cybil asked in exasperation. All night she had thought about Wren and how botched her simple attempt at intimacy and phone sex went. She had yet to find any sexual relief from the tension that was spilling over in waves and probably affecting the mood of everyone who crossed her path.

"You're actually more of a Kalinda, in my opinion, but *Good Wife* is funnier," Gloria explained with emphasized cheerful abandon as she laid down stacks of files on Cybil's desk, covering it completely, and listed the name of each case to jog Cybil's memory as she went.

"I'm not a Kalinda, either, please don't start that. The show isn't even on anymore," Cybil lamented, sipping from a fresh mug of coffee. She didn't see how she was going to get through the day's work at this rate. She had half a mind to leave the piles of paperwork on her desk and head back home, draw the blackout curtains and crawl back into bed.

"You so are a Kalinda, and not just because you're gay," Gloria ignored Cybil's irritation and continued jovially with her line of thought. "You're like Kalinda because you keep everything bottled up, you never talk—you know you gotta open up now and then or its gonna catch up to you. Tick tock."

Gloria widened her eyes comically and tapped her watch as Cybil increased the intensity of her sneer.

Cybil liked Gloria. She was the only one in the office who got away with a less than professional attitude around her, mainly because Gloria was highly organized and always completed her work assignments while garnering respect through her frankness and honest spirit. She'd bailed Cybil out of many deadline dilemmas over the years, so she had earned her place and was afforded a cocky attitude.

"Maybe I do express myself, but just not to you."

"Right, Honey, have you seen my face? Strangers on the street come up to me and tell me all kinds of personal information. I hear about prescription drug addictions, sordid divorces, and messy affairs that lead to sordid divorces, you name it. If you talked to anyone about personal stuff, you'd have talked to me by now."

"Alright, I get it—perhaps I'm not the best communicator. I don't like to talk about emotions. There. Have I admitted enough for you today?" Cybil shook her head and stared down into her coffee. Gloria was good at getting under her skin.

"Aw, but you are always pushing at everyone else in your life to spill everything. You're good at tricking people into confessing, that's why your win rate is so high in court."

Cybil blinked as she considered the truth bombs that Gloria was laying down.

"Gloria, close the door for a minute, please." She had a feeling she was going to regret this.

"You know Wren's been away for a long time, and…I can't believe I'm about to tell you this…"

"Let it out, lady," Gloria encouraged as her full cheeks pulled upward into a self-congratulatory smirk.

Cybil inhaled through her mouth and shifted her eyes up to the ceiling.

"I tried to initiate some…hot talk over the phone last night and she got really upset. Like I don't know if we're still together."

"You tried to have phone sex with your girlfriend and it got that bad? Shit," Gloria nodded. "Okay, do you have her current address? First thing I'm going to do is send her flowers from you as an apology."

"Why do I have to apologize?" Cybil barked. She was still angry and honestly didn't see any fault on her part. She steadied herself and reacted to Gloria's look of condemnation, "Um, okay, yeah, flowers—lots of flowers."

"Next, this is what you're going to do, head down to Michigan Avenue at lunch and go to La Perla, buy some fancy panties in Wren's favorite color. Spare no expense and make sure you get measured for proper bra fit, sometimes those heavy boobs of yours are looking saggy—pardon me for saying so."

Cybil looked down at her chest and narrowed her eyes, but refrained from commenting. She had bigger things than her boobs weighing on her.

"Gloria, do you and Ron have, you know, um—" Cybil grasped to say the words.

"Phone sex? Yeah, but it's different with a man. All I text him is that when I get home I'm gonna unzip his pants, take it on out, and suck on it. And we are off to the races, if you catch my drift."

"Ew," Cybil did not want to know that, but supposed she had set herself up. She just could not imagine texting those words to Wren. It wasn't even applicable to lesbians. She cleared her throat.

"Once I buy this expensive lingerie what am I

supposed to do with it?"

"Easy now, I'm going to get you something special delivered tonight. Promise you'll use it?" Gloria winked. "Forget the phone sex, get on Skype. Skype sex is where it's at. Put on Wren's favorite music, and show her that sexy lingerie and that sexy you. Just go with the flow. You have to make the effort, that's the essential ingredient to a happy relationship."

Cybil mulled this idea over and decided that desperate times called for desperate measures.

She thought back to how she'd first met Wren. It was a rainy afternoon and Cybil was waiting at Argo Tea for her girlfriend at the time, a law professor at Loyola, to meet her for a coffee date. A crowd of students had come into the small café to escape the cold rain and there were no open tables. Wren had asked if she could sit down with Cybil for a minute to organize her papers. The older woman had felt an instant attraction to the sweet student as they struck up a conversation.

When she told Wren that she was a lawyer, the young woman's eyes had lit up in wonder, and Cybil realized how beautiful she was despite being drenched from the rain. She offered her jacket and felt the need to help Wren slip into it—an excuse to get closer to her. She wasn't even a little bit upset when her ex-girlfriend texted that she had to cancel their date, because Cybil had found much better company.

She learned that Wren was about to graduate from her journalism Master's program and Cybil offered to help her network with some of her business connections. It was a great excuse to give Wren her phone number, and from that moment on, the pair had been inseparable.

When Cybil came back to the present from the

banks of her memories, Gloria was staring at her with a conspiratorial grin. Cybil took a long sip from her coffee and smiled, "Do you really think this is going to work?"

"I know it will," Gloria said as she left the office to put the plan into action.

※ ※ ※ ※

Cybil decided to walk back to her apartment that afternoon, armed with a shopping bag from La Perla, which held a racy, royal blue intricate lace bra and panty set with matching garters and stockings. It was a long walk home, back to her Gold Coast apartment, but she needed to burn off the excess nervous energy that had been brewing all day. Her phone buzzed with a message from Gloria letting her know that the flowers had been delivered.

When Cybil got home, she found a small yellow and pink box sitting on the floor right outside her door. She picked it up as she unlocked the door and walked inside. She hung up her coat and set down her bags, eager to find out what Gloria had sent to her. She slid her fingernail underneath the tape that sealed the box and opened it up to find a note that read, "From Slippery Tulips, A women only intimate boutique." Inside, encased in velvet, was a vibrator.

"Of course," Cybil smiled and rotated the intensity dial, surprised that it was fully loaded with fresh batteries. The toy buzzed to life and an intense shiver ran through Cybil's sexually deprived body. This plan was either going to crash and burn or sail on spectacularly, but Cybil was committed either way. The rest of it was up to Wren.

She poured a glass of wine and decided to eat something, as her stomach was sour from too much coffee and not enough food. As she was preparing some pasta, her phone rang again. This time it was Wren, and the message was positive.

"Hey, I got the flowers. Love them! Thank you so much. I'm sorry about yesterday. I overreacted."

Cybil took her opportunity to strike while the iron was hot, "Let's forget about it. Would you be available to get on Skype in about an hour?"

"Sure, I just woke up, and the flowers were at my door. I don't have any meetings today," Wren replied instantly. It was on. Cybil finished dinner, brushed her teeth and took a quick shower. She always felt sexier when she was clean. She styled her hair and did her makeup, except, unlike a normal date, getting dressed ended with the underwear.

The lingerie was a perfect fit and she was glad that she got over her embarrassment about getting her bust measured. She took a step back when she had finished fixing the garter belt to her thigh-high stockings and looked in the mirror. With a sigh of approval, she readied the toy in the middle of her bed, and flipped through her iTunes collection looking for music that would get Wren excited. If this was going to work she had to go all in and change her attitude.

"Lady Gaga it is," Cybil said to herself, chuckling at her girlfriend's undying love for the eccentric pop star.

"Whatever works was Wren's motto in life, love and work.

Cybil was praying that this would do the trick. She heard the burbling Skype tone, signaling that Wren was calling and her nerves shifted into high gear. She answered immediately and projected an air of confidence despite fighting feelings of doubt.

She was wearing her maroon silky robe with the belt tied loosely around her waist and the top was loose and gaping, so Wren could see that there was something tantalizing going on underneath, but without giving away the full sight of her toned body and the sexy lingerie.

"Wow, you look gorgeous." Wren said. She was smiling beautifully and full of affection. Cybil was hit with a hard pang of longing. She wanted to hold her and kiss her so badly.

"You look stunning, my love," Cybil responded enthusiastically, taking in as much as she could through the screen of her iPad. She could see the vase full of yellow tulips sitting on the dresser to the side of Wren's bed as the morning light filtered in.

"What are you wearing?" Wren pushed her face closer to the screen as she tried to get her own look at Cybil.

"Not much, honestly. I was kind of hoping we'd have a hot Skype date," Cybil blushed a bit, as her cheeks flushed in fear and anticipation. The last thing she wanted was a repeat of last night's disaster.

"That's the plan? Are you going to let me see what's under that robe?" Wren's eyes were shining with mischief.

"If you're good," Cybil teased and lifted her eyebrow as she pulled back the edge of the robe just enough for Wren to catch sight of her delectable cleavage for a moment before snapping it closed.

"I'll be good,' Wren assured her in earnest. Her voice dropped as she added, "I thought about yesterday and I want to make you happy. I was being selfish, so if you want to talk about fantasies, I'm game."

That was a relief to hear, but Cybil knew not to go right for the bondage and anal penetration talk. Wren needed to be eased into sex with lots of foreplay and reassurance, and phone sex—or rather Skype sex— would be no different.

"Are you sure? I don't want you to feel pressured," Cybil had to check in and make sure that this was what Wren wanted.

"Yeah, it's better that I can see you, let's just—go slow, please?" Wren asked and Cybil noticed that Wren was wearing her beloved David Bowie concert shirt. It had been a Thrift Store find, when the couple had spent a long Saturday afternoon exploring the city and the niche shop on Armitage Street. Cybil remembered that day fondly and now she noted happily that the shirt was too small and tight on Wren, especially around her chest. She could see the peaks of her nipples, stiff and pressing against the worn grey fabric.

This was a very good sign indeed. Cybil turned on Lady Gaga's *"The Edge of Glory,"* and Wren bounced merrily on her bed, "What's this?"

She didn't answer with words. Instead she untied her belt and slowly pulled her robe off her shoulders so Wren could see the lingerie.

"God, you're hot! Royal blue is my favorite color," Wren peered at her curiously as Cybil lifted her chin and made sure that she was positioned at a flattering angle for the camera.

"All I've been thinking about today is you, Wren. I picked this out and hoped that you'd like me in it."

"I love it," Wren confirmed and then trailed off as Cybil boldly caressed her breasts, plucking lightly at her nipples. She was surprised at how erotic it felt to be performing for the camera and knowing her girlfriend was watching.

"What are you thinking about? Tell me," Wren pleaded, and although it was difficult, Cybil opened up.

"I'm thinking about how strange it is that you're halfway across the world and I'm touching my body, letting you watch. Imagining your tongue on my breasts, stroking over my nipples again and again, until you can't help but to suck on them sharply, and make me gasp." Cybil pulled the cups of her bra down, exposing herself without caution, her only aim to get her fingers on her bare breasts. She was really going through with this, and the further she went the easier it got.

Remembering that she had a vibrator to help speed the events along, she held it up to show Wren, "Look what I have. I've never understood why you never let me use one of these on you?"

"Are you going to use that on yourself?" Wren asked with unabashed wonder.

"You bet I am," Cybil said as she turned it on, touching the tip of the toy to her right nipple. She breathed in deeply as pricks of pleasurable sensation coursed through her body. "You do want to watch, don't you?"

"Yes," Wren responded to the question with enthusiasm and then answered Cybil's first one. "I never really masturbate much. I was raised with a healthy sense of Catholic guilt, and vibrators were evil."

"We must work on getting that notion out of your head, why don't you just watch, hmm?" Cybil felt spurred on by that same guilty look she often saw on Wren's face. "Or maybe you could mirror my movements…you look very warm, take off your shirt."

To her surprise her girlfriend did as she was told without fanfare. She pulled her shirt over her head. The sight of her girlfriend's nude torso pleased Cybil. Perfectly sized breasts sat high on her chest, punctuated by her pretty pink nipples.

"Good, play with your nipples like this," Cybil resumed her own ministrations, and they silently watched each other.

Wren ran her palms over her breasts and mimicked what Cybil was doing.

For a moment, Cybil's concentration was broken. She was so happy that this was working. Skype was marvelous for closing the distance between them, and Wren was finally agreeable.

"You don't need to feel guilty about this, I'm right here with you," Cybil encouraged her sensing Wren was becoming a bit self-conscious. It was time to take it to the next level. Cybil scooted back in bed, giving Wren a wider view. She spread her legs and let her see the sexy thigh high stockings and the lacy underwear that she wore in full view.

"When you've pleasured yourself before, I know you said you didn't do it much, but when you did— how did you like to do it? Did you lay on your back and rub your clit, or on your stomach and finger yourself?" It was risky to ask such direct questions, but they had cultivated a safe space, and Wren was into it.

"When I was in college, I wasn't out of the closet yet, and my roommate always had her boyfriend over to the dorms. I'd feel awkward so I'd go to the study lounge in the basement late at night sometimes. There was never anyone down there, and the door locked so

I had privacy. This is so embarrassing," Wren covered her face with her hands.

"Go on, I want to hear about it," Cybil hoped she'd keep talking.

"I liked to watch *Law and Order SVU* reruns and I had a huge crush on Mariska Hargitay. She was so hot with her swagger and her gun...Mmm," Wren said as she finally uncovered her eyes. "There was this couch there and I liked to sit on the armrest. I figured out that if I straddled it and rubbed myself on it, I'd get off."

"While thinking about Mariska Hargitay..." Cybil asked. Her mind worked to the picture of Wren doing just that, and the mental image was sexy in an innocent way. She took the vibrator and upped the intensity, then slid the tip under the waistband of her panties, softly brushing it against herself, not giving in fully, but letting her need grow as her clit throbbed and she became more aroused. She was wet and ready and she wanted Wren to know it.

"Show me?" Cybil suggested. "Take one of those pillows and straddle it. Pretend it's my face that you're riding. Hump the shit out of it."

Wren closed her eyes and shuddered. She grabbed a pillow and put it down in front of the camera, while Cybil quickly unclipped her garter belt and slid her panties over her hips and down her legs. She watched as Wren dutifully straddled the firm pillow and started to swirl her hips rhythmically against it.

"How does it feel?" She asked as Wren opened her eyes and watched with a trancelike, dreamy gaze as Cybil spread her lips with the vibrator and slid it slowly up and down softly gasping each time she slid it over her clit.

"Hmm, it's good..." Wren mumbled, churning

her hips faster, as she shifted her weight and bunched up the pillow to find the sweet spot. "Yeah, I am imagining…like you said…your face and your tongue up inside me. So good."

Wren threw her head back and squeezed her breast. She was beautiful when she let go—The edge of glory had a whole new meaning now.

"Yes, just like that, keep it up," Cybil's own voice was beginning to shake, she came close to orgasm very quickly considering how hot this was for her and how long it had been since she'd last had one. Wren cried out in a whine as she came on her pillow, signaling Cybil to give in and increase the direct pressure on her clit with the vibrator.

She followed her girlfriend with her own orgasm immediately. She rode out the waves as her body felt good and heavy with relaxation, release and a flood of endorphins. This was what she needed all along, if she couldn't have her girlfriend in the flesh. It wasn't quite the same, but she knew now that Skype was a substitute to get them through the time apart, and Wren knew how to open up when she wanted to. Gloria was so getting a raise.

Lisa Blush enjoys writing, comedy and twirling fire baton. Lisa lives in Iowa with her two spoiled dogs: a Japanese Chin named Fonzie and a Shih Tzu named Chumley.

Peter Brady

By Sallyanne Monti

March, 2000 – New York City

Contours

The day started like any other, with an all too familiar dull ache in the center of my chest and the sinking feeling that this isn't a bad dream I can wake up from, this is my life.

As I slid into my Ford Contour and headed to work via the FDR Drive, surrounded by the comfy cocoon of commuter traffic, a convergent calm enveloped me. My car is the one place I can peacefully escape into the recesses of my mind to contemplate the many facets of my broken heart.

After five years, I still haven't moved on from losing my ex-girlfriend Callie. As self-doubt consumed me, I continued to obsess over what I could of done differently and why our love wasn't enough.

In 1995, I ended a twenty-year marriage to my high school boyfriend, when I fell deeply in love with my best friend Callie. She fell just as hard for me except Callie wasn't quite out of her own twenty-five year marriage to her husband Rick. Nor was she convinced that she wanted to live life as a lesbian. In the final analysis, Rick and her marriage won out and our love that would conquer all, didn't.

And so it went for months into years, the right of passage and stages of grief in the interminable process of healing my broken heart. I cursed, I cried, I prayed, I hoped. When all else failed, I broke things, mostly all the things she ever gave me. I cried so much I had to replace my contact lenses with eyeglasses. I swore so much that my Brooklyn accent, the one I'd worked so hard to eradicate, came back with a vengeance. I broke down and wrote Callie love letters that I later tossed into my bottom nightstand drawer, unsent. I returned to breaking whatever things of hers I'd sworn I would keep forever, until nothing was left—well almost nothing—I kept a small silver angelfish charm, the first gift she had ever given me.

Then one day, on a day like any other, in the midst of my ongoing misery, it happened. Right there in my Ford Contour in the middle of commuter traffic, I moved on. As my car crawled down the FDR Drive past the United Nations, the self-pity I'd been wallowing in turned to humiliation. Along with the acceptance that Callie no longer wanted me came the sudden realization that I had made a giant fool of myself trying to force her to choose me over her long-term marriage.

I kept my love for Callie alive by enfolding the pain of my broken heart tucked away deep inside me. When I was missing Callie, I'd find a quiet place and retreat. I'd carefully take out one little remembrance at a time, unwrapping it slowly, savoring every treasured memory, and ultimately reliving every agonizing minute of our lost relationship. This propensity to live in the past became my new obsession, one that was readily available in the deep recesses of my mind and the tortured chambers of my heart.

Without warning, in June of 2000, that love was unexpectedly set free on the FDR Drive in New York City. I suddenly felt as light as the fluffy white clouds in the sky and as clear as the bright, sunny day. With an open heart and newfound excitement, I spent a most glorious and restful commute home.

Beneath the Surface

Finally home, I kicked off my high heel dress shoes just inside the front door. They slid across the foyer stopping a few inches shy of the dark wood double-door aquarium stand. I love my fish tank. I could stare at it for hours in my cozy black leather recliner in the giant foyer of my craftsman-style home. As an outsider looking in—everything appears crystal clear—in the bubbles there is life—within the colors there is brilliance—within the magnified images is a revealing light of hope—and below the ambiguous waves of the waterline, all is right with the world.

I am a Pisces, with the ability to see things beneath the surface while gravitating towards the holy trinity of water signs—Cancers, other Pisces, and Scorpios. As I acknowledged that Callie was a Scorpio, an unexplainable inclination crossed my mind, insinuating there might be a Cancer in my near future. *This is ridiculous*, I thought as I picked up my shoes and headed into the kitchen, pushing aside the nagging gut feeling.

It's Time to Change

I shook my head to clear my thoughts as I dropped the mail on the counter, opened the fridge and grabbed an ice-cold sparkling water. I felt my stomach grumble and realized it'd been a long time since I felt alive enough to have an appetite. Even a frozen dinner entrée was appealing. I popped a Lean Cuisine Chicken and Broccoli into the microwave, and changed into sweats and a T-shirt. With my morning coffee long gone I couldn't blame the jittery feeling and strange humming in my chest on too much caffeine. *What is going on today? Is Mercury in retrograde?* I thought.

The microwave beeped, interrupting my thoughts and alerting me that my frozen healthy dinner option was ready. The beeping reminded me of a few days earlier, when in this very kitchen my friend Pat passionately lectured me to get on with my life and join the dating website she swore would lead me to the love of my life. We stood in front of this microwave waiting for our expanding bag of Orville Redenbacher to stop popping so we could celebrate my birthday— watching my favorite movie of all time, *A Very Brady Christmas*—while stuffing handfuls of salty puffed kernels into our mouths.

Pat turned me towards her, grabbed me by the shoulders and looking into my eyes said, "Sammy, how many years are you going to keep your life on hold. You're young, attractive, brilliant, financially secure, and funny as shit. Are you going to throw away the best years of your life on a lost love? It's your thirty-seventh birthday. When are you going to wake up and move on."

I rolled my eyes at Pat and at the name of the dating website she had suggested earlier, Oneandonly-dot-com.

"Come on Pat. Who in their right mind believes in

one and only anymore? Besides I haven't been on a date in twenty-two years, since I was fifteen years old."

"Well then it's about time you go on a date my friend," Pat responded. "You've wasted enough of your life pining over Callie, your number one obsession. This is your year. I'm calling it the year of the Brady, named for your second biggest obsession, The Brady Bunch." She tossed the wrapped gift to me while enunciating "Happy Birthday Sammy I love you. I hope this gift takes you back to your inner child so you can stop being so serious and have some fun."

"I love you too Pat. What is this?" I said while waving the wrapped gift in my right hand.

"Which one of those polyester-clad dorks is your favorite Brady?" Pat asked as she watched me tear open the gift.

"Peter Brady. His melodious-pubescent-crackling-girly-voice makes me downright giddy," I said, laughing. I couldn't believe my eyes as I looked down at the now unwrapped gift in my hand, 'A Very Brady Christmas' DVD. I was ecstatic and smiling.

"I can't explain it Pat," Peter's voice just does something to me, when clearly the rest of him doesn't. I'm attracted to women—but...in my favorite Brady episode Peter sounds so girly. He sings a totally lame song called 'It's Time to Change,' while his voice changes and honks it's way through several musical octaves. His crackling falsetto gives me chills." I began singing the lyrics in my fake Peter Brady voice, "When it's Time to Change, you have to rearrange...la-la-la-la-la-la-la-la-la-la."

Pat refused to join in as we both laughed.

"I think that's my new mantra," I said.

"Okay Sammy, go find your Peter Brady girl. It's

Time to Change baby, it's time to change."

My One and Only

I smiled at that birthday memory, as I plopped my Lean Cuisine on the kitchen table and sat down to open the cover of my laptop. I took a deep breath and typed in www.oneandonly.com and then created my profile under women seeking women. I giggled when my photo uploaded and thought to myself, *Sammy you just seriously shrunk your dating pool by posting that ridiculous profile pic.* There I stood with a dorky smile on my face in front of my beloved bubbling fish tank while proudly hugging my *A Very Brady Christmas* DVD.

Maybe the future love of my life is a Brady fanatic too, I thought. *Yeah...sure...right—And maybe Peter Brady is going to knock on my door singing, 'It's Time to Change,' in all his pubescent-falsetto-girl-voice glory.*

I shoved a forkful of Chicken and Broccoli into my mouth as I contemplated writing my online dating ad.

I settled on:

Sam Tessel, Pisces, age thirty-seven, born and raised in Brooklyn (don't hold it against me), Harvard grad (no kidding), super duper biz consultant (so what I drive a Ford Contour), living in NYC, love Pizza (cheese please, I'm a purest), walks on the beach (enough said), intimate conversations (about anything and everything), uproarious laughter (whether you join me or not) and kissing (for hours). Did I say kissing? I really, really love kissing.

I let the Brady pic speak for itself and pressed

the submit button. *Had I really just signed up to cruise lesbians on the internet?* I suppose I had. I was petrified and more excited than I'd been in years. Still feeling the jitters, I couldn't shake the feeling that something major was about to happen.

The next night after work while waiting for my microwaved Weight Watchers' pizza to cool off, I signed into my One and Only account. I was shocked to see that someone had sent me a virtual wink. As I clicked through to her profile, my eyes were drawn to the stranger's round adorable smiling face and the light green eyes staring back at me. Her short blonde hair was perfectly styled in a sweeping side-part. In her photo, she wore a bright pink collared golf shirt and matching plaid shorts. She looked fit, trim, and happy holding her pitching wedge in her right hand and giving a thumbs up with her left. Her eyes seemed alive and vibrant and her smile genuine.

I felt a sense of excitement as I began reading her profile summary. It read:

Jessica Ann Morgan, age thirty-three, women's golf pro, laugh nut, beach bum, born July 3rd (smack in the middle of six girls).

"OMG, a Cancer!" I exclaimed aloud in my kitchen.

I eagerly moved past her profile summary to read her ad:

Dear Soul mate:

I know you're out there searching for me as I am for you. I can feel it. I know you are caring, passionate, funny, and honest. I'm a sensitive, witty romantic who still believes in forever. I have a kind, compassionate heart, which will only be given to you.

I'm looking forward to frolicking on the beach, having deep interesting conversations and joking around and having fun. I look forward to hearing from you.

PS I love The Brady Bunch and I love kissing.

PSS I love kissing while watching The Brady Bunch even more!

Waiting for you.

Boston, MA

Brady Bunch and kissing, she's perfect...but Boston? I felt my heart sink. *That's hundreds of miles away. Shit!*

I pushed aside the nagging possibility that I might wind up nursing yet another broken heart while drowning in the challenges of a long distance relationship, but jumped in feet first and wrote her back—secretly hoping we could write a fanfic-Brady-themed-happily-ever-after-ending of our own.

Dear Boston:

Was it One and Only's website algorithms, a Brady-twisted act of fate, or just pure coincidence that linked our profiles together? Ahh...what a shame...the perfect woman...you said all the right things. I could say them all right back at you. It was all right and all good until you got to the Boston part. I'm a New York City girl. Wanna be pen pals?

Signed,

Sam in NYC

Despite my better judgment, I took this dating thing one step further and downloaded the One and Only Dating App onto my cellphone. I then proceeded to obsessively check my account for a reply from Ms. Boston—or a wink, poke, slap or whatever it is that one does in response—for the better part of three nerve-wracking days. I was in denial about my propensity for compulsive behavior and told myself I was simply acting appropriately for a person in the early stages of meeting someone new, as I checked my cellphone App for the hundredth time that day before going to sleep. Oh well, I guess she didn't like me after all.

On day four, she wrote back.

Dear NYC Sam,

Pen pals huh? Even the Brady's and their eternal optimism would question…if having a long distance pen pal is worth the inevitable chain of events that are bound to ensue…as we fall madly in love…yet hopelessly separated by hundreds of miles? Eh? What the hell, I'm game if you are.

Signed,
Your One and Only,
Jess in Boston

June, 2000
New York City and Boston, Massachusetts

You Had Me At…

I thought of that old saying—*You had me at hello.* With Jess it was—*You had me at PS I love The Brady Bunch and I love kissing.*

In that panic-stricken moment as I read these words, her words, I realized my heart had been duly awakened and unexpectedly attached to this stranger. There'd be no turning back.

We were fast, furious, fantastic, and far apart.

In the three whirlwind months since meeting, I lived for her messages and hung on her every written word. She was passionate and intense in one sentence and had me falling off my chair with laughter in the next. Our nonstop messaging and long endless emails dove deeper into our virtual exploration of each other. We had yet to meet in person, talk on the phone or Skype.

As we grew closer the reality of our long distance separation loomed ominously overhead. Albeit unsuccessfully, we took turns making sporadic attempts to back away from our growing relationship in our futile efforts to not get hurt, to protect our hearts, and to avoid the inevitable pain and estrangement of our long distance predicament.

Ignorantly, and sometimes simultaneously we teetered atop our imaginary fence of should we take it to the next level or not, believing no harm would ensue if we just remained pen pals. As much as we wanted to hear each other's voices, we were reveling in our virtual bond and teasing each other with the promise of one day, actually talking on the phone.

By the beginning of our fourth month of cybernetic dating, things got more intense. Missing Jess was barely tolerable. Connected by instant messenger and cellphone apps, the witty satires, childhood stories, and extended family antics amid serious contemplations of every imaginable subject matter, flowed easily between us. Our shared appreciation of silly 70's sitcoms, multifarious literature, Chinese chicken salads and cheese pizza drew us even closer together as we refused to acknowledge the long distance obstacle in our growing relationship.

Though never spoken aloud, it was clear to our separate groups of friends that we were deeply in love. Our refusal to speak these words to each other was a desperate attempt to hold onto what was left of our sanity and independence. We missed each other terribly. I know this because Jess would let it slip. When the nonchalance of our façade became too much to maintain, she'd say *"I miss you so much Sammy and yet I feel like I don't know enough of you yet. And I want to know you, all of you."* In my weakest moments I fantasized quitting my job, subletting my condo, packing my life into my Ford Contour, and showing up on her doorstep. It was the memory of the humiliation I felt in my one-sided relationship with Callie that stopped me dead in my tracks. I never wanted to feel like that kind of a fool ever again. In the absence of an invitation from Jess…the risk to my fragile emotions was too high.

As the months wore on, the longing to be with Jess in the same two square inches was insurmountable. Something had to change. I couldn't go on this way for much longer. Not talking about it didn't erase the reality that we had grown to be much more than pen pals.

Eventually in our fifth month of virtual dating, the obsessive and constant messaging between us, hinted at our first phone call. I allowed myself to cautiously contemplate when we might speak on the phone for the first time. Instead of openly discussing our love and angst, Jess and I continued to taunt each other using humor as our defense in a final attempt of avoidance.

As I came to terms with accepting the boundaries we'd created, Jess began to tease me unmercifully, accusing me of dodging a phone call because *"I must surely be one of those New Yorkers with a thick offensive*

84

Brooklyn accent."

I accused her of being a self-declared southern belle hiding behind her laptop in an attempt to conceal her incoherent ramblings in the dialectal oddities and clipped vowel-less tones of her deep south Mississippi roots.

Despite my assurances that I had been verbally rehabilitated and culturally cleansed of my crass Brooklyn accent—Jess insisted I would assault her ears with an onslaught of cawfee and dawg and whatz da matta wit chu's, while dropping the F-bomb every other word. Unable to convince her otherwise, I let her continue to believe she was right.

❧ ❧ ❧ ❧

September, 2000
New York City and Boston, MA

Peter Brady

We planned to speak for the first time on a sunny Saturday morning. After six months of online chatting, I was so nervous I felt my heart pounding in my throat. I tried calming myself with deep breaths. With my cell phone in one hand, I sat on the sofa contemplating the call that would make or break my future, with this adorable woman I'd come to care about.

What if she really doesn't like how I sound? What if we don't hit it off on the phone? What if after all these months of messages and emails...outside of our virtual world we just don't connect? My head wouldn't stop running ridiculous rejection scenarios. I was petrified. This was about to become very real.

As I stared into space willing myself to dial Jess'

number, I noticed my *A Very Brady Christmas* DVD on the coffee table in front of me. I picked it up examining it as if I was seeing it for the first time. Turning it around in the palms of my hands, I rubbed the shiny plastic cover hoping a Genie in the melodious voice of Peter Brady would appear, singing his one hit wonder song and my new mantra, *It's Time to Change.*

Of course, he didn't, and as I softly hummed the tune, I dialed her number. If all else failed, we could talk Brady on the call and eventually hang up while chastising ourselves for wasting the last six months of our lives avoiding this call. As I pushed send, I wondered—*Will she answer the phone? Will she think I sound crass? What will I say to her? I'm so nervous I can't think.*

On the third ring, she answered and said, "Hello Sam, it's nice to meet you, sort of."

OMG…it's her, I thought as I swallowed hard.

There in the midst of five simple letters forming a word I'd recognized a zillion times in my life was the sweetest *"Hello"* I'd ever heard.

Her voice crackled at the end of that hello. It was a sound I immediately loved. The by-product of her Mississippi roots and Massachusetts upbringing…the letter O took on a whole new tone. I felt my heart flutter in the middle of my chest, like a butterfly flapping its gentle wings as it contemplated its next move.

It was both unsettling and serene. Her melodious voice had an upward falsetto lilt and downward resonance all at the same time. Her voice was oddly familiar, and yet this was our first call. *Where have I heard this voice before?* I thought.

Then it hit me. Within the dulcet tones of her voice was the sign I'd been looking for. I smiled as the promise of this new love, enveloped me. My heart continued to flutter.

"Hi, Jess, I'm so happy to hear your voice," I said

"Well you're lucky you don't have a Brooklyn accent," Jess replied.

"After all the grief you've given me over my imaginary Brooklyn accent, you sound like Peter Brady when he was going through puberty," I said. "All this Brady talk and you forget to mention you sound like Peter Brady?"

"If you're trying to insult me, it's not working. I happen to love The Brady Bunch as you know and Peter is my favorite too," She said.

"If you're trying to get me to like you more it's working. I happen to love The Brady Bunch as you well know and Peter Brady is my one and only."

"Well he was your one and only. Now I am!" She said.

"Of course you are, how could I have forgotten that?" I asked.

"Doesn't he have the sexiest pubescent voice ever?" She said.

"Actually no, no he doesn't Jess. You do!"

I chose my next words carefully, as they would set the tone for our future.

"I can listen to your voice forever."

"I love your voice too Sammy. Why did we wait so long to speak on the phone?" Jess asked.

She loves my voice? I felt my heart skip a beat as I thought about how I wanted to respond to Jess.

As Jess' voice faded into the background, my thoughts began to run wild. I looked down at the coffee table in front of me and picked up the letter I received in today's mail and unfolded it. I ran my finger over the raised red shield shaped emblem of the Harvard University letterhead. Had it really been over two years since my grueling multi-step panel interviews in Massachusetts? After all that, Harvard had put the position on hold due to budget cuts. Having heard nothing from them since, I just stopped thinking about this position as a possibility.

Overcome with emotion, I began to tremble as I quickly reread the letter I held in my hand.

Dear Samantha Tessel:

Harvard University is devoted to excellence in teaching, learning, research and leadership. As a decorated Harvard Alumni and Internationally recognized Business Leader, we are pleased to offer you the following full-time, permanent staff position at our Cambridge Massachusetts Campus, located just 3.3 miles from metropolitan Boston, to begin in 30 days from your acceptance.

-Dean of Business Mentorship Program

The rest of the letter was a blur through the tears that streamed freely down my face. I stifled a sob as I swallowed the lump that was forming in my throat and wiped the dampness off my face with the back of my hand.

I thought about Callie and how desperately I had loved her, how much of myself I had lost in loving her, how deeply she hurt me and how long I'd pined for her...wasting over five years of my life wallowing in my own self-pity. Was I able to put myself out there again? Could I move to Cambridge for this job? Yes. It was a highly sought after position. Could I move within 3.3 miles of my one and only, risking my heart in pursuit of this new love?

Lost in my own thoughts, I vaguely heard Jess calling my name.

"Sam, Sam are you there?" She asked.

I looked at the phone, as if it could give me an answer.

"Hey, Sammy are you there? Did you hear what I said? I said I love your voice, why did we wait so long to speak on the phone?"

"Jess...I...well...Jess...uh...I...I love your voice too. But it's more than that...I...I love you! I love you Jessica Ann Morgan. I love all of you, everything about you. I love your wit, your mind...your insane sense of humor. I love your essence, your being and the brilliant facets of your very soul. Most of all, I love your heart. A heart I will treasure and care for all the days of my life, if you let me. I love you Jess, I love you."

The tears were pouring down my face again as I thought, *There, I said it. I feel it, I want it...I said it.* Despite the relief at finally having it all out in the open, I held my breath as I waited for her response.

"Sam oh Sammy, I'm so scared, I'm terrified. I love you too my darling, to the depths of my soul, in every crevice of my heart there is only you."

My heart raced as her words sunk in, yet an eerie foreboding still lingered in the back of my mind. My jitters went into overdrive, as my entire body continued to shake.

"Oh Jess, I was so afraid you didn't feel the same way," I said.

"I feel the same way Sam, I love you so much, but this is a hopeless situation. I can't leave my job. I'm on a contract with the PGA. I'm stuck here in Boston for another five years. I can't endure loving you from hundreds of miles away. I just can't do it. I need you in my life not on the outskirts of my life. I don't see how this is going to work out. We should have left things, as they were and stayed pen pals. I don't know why we tried to change everything," Jess said as she began to cry.

I put the Harvard letter back down on my coffee table, smoothed the wrinkles with the palms of my hands, snapped a picture of it with my cellphone and texted it to Jess.

I heard the ding of her phone as she asked, "Why did you text me Sammy?"

"I texted you our future my love. As Peter Brady says, 'when it's time to change you have to rearrange.' I love you so much, Jess. I love you beyond reason. Please read the text."

I heard Jess gasp into the phone as I imagined her trying to read the tiny texted version of my Harvard job offer letter. Her cries turned into sobs.

"Oh Sammy…I…I…I love you too, more than you know. Come to me my love, come now," She said.

And we burst into laughter as we both began to sing…her in her Peter Brady voice and me in my faux Brooklyn accent voice…"when it's time to change, you have to rearrange, la-la-la-la-la-la-la-la-la."

Sallyanne Monti is an author and editor. Her fiction and non-fiction short stories, articles, poems and edited pieces appear in numerous anthologies, magazines and newspapers. In her spare time she plays guitar and composes music. She lives in Palm Springs California with her wife Mickey and their doggies Sola and Zorra.
Website: www.sallyannemonti.com

The Daughter of War

By K. A. Masters

Penthesilea entered the Trojan gates at dawn, bloody spear in hand. The townsfolk welcomed her and her companions with excitement. Many of them had never seen an Amazon before, and they flocked to touch her armor, braids, and bloodstained hands in wonder. Still mourning the loss of their beloved Prince Hector, the Trojans clung to her like a starving man clings to his last loaf of bread.

The Amazon queen smiled back at them, infected by their excitement as they led her to King Priam's hall. As she traveled, she tried to ignore the terrible condition of their city. The faces that greeted her were only boys and old men. No youths joined them. The women, too, escorted her with no infants at their side, no breasts swollen with milk. The few children that she saw merely shuffled in the streets, too frail and underfed to find the energy to play.

The decade-long siege did not leave the palace untouched. The royal guard welcomed her in the main hall, brandishing gilded spears and armor in an opulent display. When she left the main hall, all of the other chambers were bare. Her dinner was prepared from the last of the salted pork from the larder and heated with ornately carved wood that had once belonged to a royal bedpost.

When King Priam beheld her, he found his joy again. Falling to his knees and clasping her, the old man pressed his face into her stomach and wept, clinging to her with ferocious desperation. His wife Hecuba looked on in shock, holding her eight-year-old daughter Polyxena against her in a protective embrace. Her other hand held back the wild Kassandra, restraining the mad princess as she raved about horses and firebrands.

When the king had found an end to his weeping, Penthesilea gently gathered him in her arms and helped him find the strength to rise, being careful to not pinch his aged skin in the joints of scale armor on her sleeves.

"Welcome, dear child," he smiled, doting on her as if she were his own son. "Home again at last! My greatest ally! My own sweet Penthesilea!" he frothed, squeezing her forearm in encouragement.

"Many thanks for the kind welcome, Majesty," Penthesilea spoke with dignity, hoping to keep the king from resuming his vigilance of sorrow.

"A homecoming feast fit for a king—for a victorious king! Servants, come! Slaughter the finest bull we have—we shall dine on steaks tonight!"

"Majesty, we have no more bulls," one of the kitchen maids dared to speak.

"Then a ram! We dine on mutton!" Priam countered.

"But there's no..." she began, but Penthesilea interrupted her, hoping to spare her host further embarrassment.

"No need for a feast tonight, Majesty," the Amazon bowed, "Your servants have already fed me a supper fit for my royal appetite. And forgive my companions for not being here to join in the revelry—they have already left the palace, desirous to visit their friends in the city and enjoy their company again. They shall rejoin me in the morning to fight—we do not need any feasts tonight."

"Very well, I suppose," Priam sighed. "But what gift can I give you? What reward can I offer? You are risking your life in aiding our cause. All who have faced Achilles have failed. My own son Hector…" his voice faltered, and Queen Hecuba placed a hand on his shoulder in comfort.

"Give me lodgings for the night, my King. And in the morning, I shall fight the mighty Achilles, cut a path through your Greek enemies, and burn their ships to the ground. I vow it." Penthesilea swore, hand over her leather-covered heart.

"How naïve!" A voice behind her spat out.

She turned to find Princess Andromache standing behind her, holding her child Astyanax to her breast. Having lost her husband, Andromache now clung to their child, afraid to put him down lest she lose him, too. Her hair was tangled and dirty, her clothes disheveled and torn. The only clean parts of her body were twin streaks on her cheeks where the tears have cleansed their path as they fell.

"Why are you boasting with such lies?" Andromache spat viciously, "You have not yet tried your spear against Achilles. He is the son of a goddess!"

"And I am the daughter of a god," Penthesilea countered.

"My husband Hector was the bravest warrior this land had seen. For ten long years he defended us from the Greek invaders. But Achilles—gods damn him—cut him down like a newborn lamb. We watched as he tied my Hector's still breathing body to his chariot and dragged the life out of him. Three times that monster dragged my Hector's body around the city walls. Three times I had to watch while my man choked on dirt, as he died facedown in disgrace. And I see it—I still see it when I close my eyes!" She wept, clutching her son to her chest hard enough that the infant squirmed in pain. "My husband could not defend this town, but you can?"

"Andromache, hush!" Priam scolded his daughter-in-law, desperately trying to shield his guest from her offensive words, but Penthesilea merely gave a sad smile.

"The gods do not owe us victories. We fight every day, and some days we die. Your husband died with honor in a fair fight. I am truly sorry that your Hector has fallen to Achilles. But, daughter of Aetion, I will fight with all of my strength for you and your family."

"You think you can kill Achilles?" Andromache sneered. "You and your twelve Amazons?"

"No. I am not here to kill Achilles. I am here to merely rout him until reinforcements arrive. Milord," she turned to Priam, "I bear you good news. The Ethiopian prince Memnon and his armies will arrive in a matter of days. He brings you food and troops to help you resist this terrible siege."

"Huzzah!" Priam clapped his hands in joy. "Great news!"

"And you think you can rout Achilles?" Andromache sneered.

"Of course," Penthesilea replied, "For the life of one of my dearest companions depends on it." She took Andromache's free hand in her own bloodied one and kissed it reverently.

"Milady Penthesilea, do you know our daughter-in-law?" Priam asked, alert to the gesture.

"Aye," the Amazon whispered. "Many long years ago—before the war, when we were little more than children—my sister and I visited the House of Aetion. Andromache was one of my truest companions. My sister," her face fell in sorrow as she spoke the name of her lost loved one, "Hippolyte and I had hoped that she would join us as an Amazon, but I suppose fate intended her to find a happy life with your crown prince. I have come to fight for Troy, because Troy is where my truest sister resides."

"I am glad that you are well acquainted," Priam replied, talking over the widowed princess as if she were not still present. "I had hoped her words did not offend you."

"She is a dear friend, and she speaks in sorrow. I know how little hope you have seen the past few months. But I have come to change that." Her eyes met Andromache's as she spoke. "I vow it."

"And we welcome your aid, dear one," Priam said. "Ladies," he called the various servants around him, "escort Penthesilea to her quarters. When the dawn comes, clothe her in the armor of Hector, so that our people can once more know what it's like to fight under the royal crest of Troy."

Andromache gave a steely look and left. Her handmaidens dutifully complied with their king's wishes. Guiding their guest to the royal bedchambers, they stripped Penthesilea's armor from her tired limbs, draping them on a wooden rack beside Hector's. Before they left, they filled a washbasin with warm water and brought in towels and a fresh change of clothes. And that night Penthesilea readied herself to sleep in the empty chamber of one of Priam's lost sons.

☙❧☙❧

Penthesilea was kneeling by the washbasin, staring into her bloodstained hands, when she heard a knock at her door.

Andromache entered with her slumbering son. Her eyes were still red from angry tears.

Penthesilea bowed. "I am so sorry, Andromache."

"Why are you here?" she spat.

"I too have lost the one I care about. There is nothing left for me—but the ashes of our old love."

"I heard that you slew your sister," Andromache replied, softening. "I can't imagine it was done in anger. What happened?"

She looked down at her bloodstained hands. "A boar hunt. Hippolyte jumped in the path of my spear to avoid its tusk."

Andromache took the Amazon's hand in her free one, marveling at its color. "It was an accident. You didn't do it on purpose."

"But she is dead nonetheless," she breathed. "Come with me. I can take you both away from this place." She squeezed the slumbering infant's foot affectionately, marveling at his miniscule toes.

"I can't," Andromache replied. "This is my family now. They have loved me and cared for me. And I love them, too. I won't abandon them."

"Then I will stay and fight for them," Penthesilea replied.

"No," the princess insisted. "You have to leave."

"I'm not leaving you."

"Please, go!"

"Why?"

"I can't lose you, too." She sighed. "Achilles has taken my father, my brothers, and now my husband. I'm surrounded by death and I can't endure it anymore. You need to leave this place before Achilles takes you away from me, too."

"I'm not leaving without you, Andromache. We both know how this war will end. You know what happens after a siege—what will happen to your son. What happens to women after war."

"Slavery," she spat.

"Much worse than slavery," Penthesilea countered. "Can you still fight?"

Andromache shook her head. "My fighting instinct is gone. All these years, without proper food and exercise—I do not have the physical ability to fight."

"But you can still wield a knife?"

"I haven't slaughtered a pig in years. The Trojans are more traditional. They don't allow princesses to participate in harvest."

"But you still remember how?"

Andromache nodded.

"It's no different than slaughtering a pig. Slice the throats of the Greek invaders. And, if times are desperate, slice your own."

She looked down at her slumbering son in her arms. "I can't. I can't leave my son. I can't leave my family behind."

"You might need to wield a blade to keep your son safe," the Amazon countered.

"I am not allowed to have a weapon," Andromache replied. "Priam thinks that if the women are armed, they will act out in desperation."

Penthesilea groaned in aggravation. "You don't even have a dagger to protect yourself?"

"No. It is forbidden."

Penthesilea rolled her eyes.

"I told you—things are more traditional here. This isn't the hall of my father. Aetion was a lord—but he was also a pig farmer. Priam is a king and just a king. He doesn't even fight as a soldier anymore. He advises and he orders. Nothing else."

"Well, that will change. Here," she replied, unwrapping the bindings on her bloodied spear to remove the blade from the shaft. Once it was free, she rewrapped the leather thongs around its handle to create a more comfortable grip on the weapon. "Take this, and keep it with you at all times. Hide it in your clothes or weave it in your braids."

Andromache marveled at the weapon in her former lover's hands. She took the crusted blade from Penthesilea's stained hands and dared to ask, "Is this from…?"

"Hippolyte's. I couldn't bear to wash it off."

"And your hands? You refuse to wash your sister's blood from your hands?"

"Washing is penitence. And I cannot forgive myself," the Amazon explained.

"That is foolish."

Penthesilea playfully tugged a stray lock of Andromache's disheveled hair with her bloodied hand. "And how long has it been since you've bathed? Do you think that if you stink strongly enough, it will bring your Hector back?"

"I suppose I am being foolish, too," she smiled sadly. "We both need a bath. Here," she continued, placing her slumbering son in the hollow of his father's shield, using his armor as a makeshift bassinette.

"I will wash your hands," the princess continued, pouring oil over them and gently cleansing the dirt from her cracked palms. She continued to massage and clean her hands until even the dirt beneath the Amazon's fingernails was removed. Only when the stain was gone completely did she rinse the lather away.

Penthesilea lifted her clean hand to cup Andromache's cheek, and pulled her into a kiss.

Andromache stiffened uncomfortably. "I'm different now. I have a husband, and a child...I have this life now."

"Andromache," she breathed, undone.

"I have a husband now. I love my husband."

"I know," Penthesilea smiled sadly. "But I will always treasure the time we had together, and my feelings for you will never change."

Andromache embraced her longtime companion and murmured, "I have missed you."

"And I have missed you," Penthesilea replied. "But you stink. Get into the bath. Leave this grief behind—for a night. I assure you, it will still be here waiting for you in the morning."

She chuckled and pulled off her clothes, entering the bathtub with a delightful groan.

"The water is still warm," she cooed as the Amazon washed the soot from her hair.

"How long has it been? Since you've bathed?" Penthesilea smiled as she rinsed the soap from the princess' hair.

"Two months. Two uncomfortable, itchy months," Andromache answered, scrubbing the dirt from her skin. "Hector is—was—my everything, my only. Father married me to him a month before the

Greeks overtook our village. Hector whisked me away from my home—and a month later, I was burying my father and brothers."

"Do you think your father knew that the Greeks would destroy your home on their path to Troy?"

"He knew the war was coming, and he wanted to keep me safe." She glanced to her son sleeping in the hollow of her husband's shield. "He never met his grandson."

"Aetion was a good man—but enough of the past. Our ghosts will haunt us in the morning. I beg you, let us enjoy this night without their company."

Penthesilea helped Andromache step out of the tub and wrapped her in a towel, following her to a brazier to warm herself as she dried.

"This will hurt," she apologized as she began to brush out the tangles in the princess' hair. As quickly and painlessly as she could, she brushed and braided Andromache's dark locks, and arranged them to hold the spear point.

"Feel this," Penthesilea directed her, bringing Andromache's hands up to her head to explore the pattern. "The dagger is completely covered in your braids. Arrange your hair this way, and you will never need to worry about how to protect yourself. Draw the blade out this way," she said, as she helped Andromache's fingers find the handle and extricate it.

Andromache smiled. "Aye. Thank you." She sat by the flames and watched as the Amazon took her bath.

"You still look the same," Andromache noted as Penthesilea scrubbed the dust from her travels off of her skin. "You're taller, but you haven't lost any muscle."

"You're still as beautiful as I remember," Penthesilea shot back, rising from the washbasin and grabbing a towel to dry herself.

Andromache's towel had fallen and pooled in her lap, and now she self-consciously tried to rearrange it to cover her breasts. "Motherhood has changed me," she lamented.

"Motherhood has made you more beautiful," Penthesilea countered. "Don't regret your past."

Again the princess' eyes flittered to the image of her sleeping son. "He will be my only," she said with wistful regret.

"There was a time when you said I was your only, daughter of Aetion," Penthesilea smirked, gently grabbing Andromache's towel and dropping it to the floor. "Let's go to bed."

Andromache settled into bed beside Penthesilea, lying in the positions that their many nights together had made them accustomed to. Andromache laid her head upon the scar on Penthesilea's chest, where her breasts had been removed when she had entered service to the Amazon at the end of her girlhood. The asymmetry was jarring but beautiful. Andromache kissed her lover's flat chest and settled her ear against it, listening to the rhythm of her heartbeat.

"Do you regret it? Do you miss them?" Andromache asked, tracing the scar delicately with her fingers.

"No," she said with a sigh.

"Such a barbaric sacrifice to join the Sisters!" Andromache marveled. "Does it really help in battle to such an extent that it justifies the pain?"

"It is necessary, Andromache," she replied. "It's the only way to survive the curse. The women in my clan who don't make the sacrifice at puberty fill up with tumors and die."

Her eyes widened. "All of them?"

"All of them," she confirmed. "It was painful, but I'd rather be alive with no breasts than dead and bountiful." Penthesilea sighed and countered with a playful poke. "Did this hurt?"

"Puberty?" she asked, coyly.

"Birthing," the Amazon clarified. "Weaning. Motherhood."

"Of course. But it was worth it." Andromache sighed. "But I am so afraid."

"I am afraid for you. But I vow I'll keep you safe."

"Even though I am another man's wife?" she countered. "Even though I've given him children?"

"I will never give you children," Penthesilea joked, then grew serious. "I never wanted your whole heart, I just wanted to be part of your life."

"And I want you to leave this place. This will not end well for you."

"How do you know?" Penthesilea said.

"Kassandra."

"The raving teenager? The one who won't shut up about horses and fire?"

"Sometimes her prophecies are true. She predicted the death of Hector."

"She predicted that a warrior would fall in battle? That's one of only two possible outcomes," Penthesilea scoffed.

"She told me that I would outlive all that I loved. That she saw me in a land called Italy, crying over two tombs."

"Two?" she inquired.

"One for Hector, and one for Astyanax. Don't you

see? You won't die here—because you aren't destined to stay and fight. I'm not destined to mourn you."

"What if she sees you crying in Italy, with me by your side? The twin tombs could represent your husband and father."

"No. I'm sorry, Penthesilea. Please—just go. Take Hector's armor and go home. Memnon will protect us."

"But—"

"Please, just go and be safe."

Penthesilea sighed. "Very well, my love."

❧❧❧❧

At dawn Penthesilea and Andromache rose from their bed and prepared for the coming battle. Andromache helped dress her love in Hector's armor, lacing the greaves and bracers around her limbs protectively. She placed the shield upon the Amazon's back and carefully belted the baldric over her chest. She kissed first Penthesilea, then the helmet that balanced on her brow.

"Do not return," Andromache said. "Please, I beg you."

The royal family assembled to offer their encouragement and gratitude as the Amazon stood before the palace's great hall and prepared to leave. A twelve-year-old boy haphazardly dressed in armor much too big for him sauntered up to join her.

"I will fight by your side," he asserted.

"Deiphobus!" Queen Hecuba cried, exasperated. "You are not ready for battle, sweet child."

Recognition lit the Amazon's face. "This is Deiphobus, Helen's new husband?"

"Yes. With Paris dead, Deiphobus is the eldest son. He has married the widowed Helen," Hecuba replied awkwardly. It was clear by the child's age that the marriage was in name only, done to keep Helen from being forced to return to the Greeks.

"My lord," Penthesilea said, trying to keep a serious face, "you need to stay behind and protect your family. Stand your guard by the palace gates, in case I have to fall back in retreat. Then you can have your chance at Achilles."

"Very well," the child said, pouting in disappointment.

Andromache left the crowd, not daring to say goodbye to her former lover. Priam gave the Amazon a fatherly kiss of affection, and his wife Hecuba repeated the gesture.

Kassandra, however, gave the Amazon words of warning. "One day they will sing songs about you. But all the songs will be sad."

"I have no doubt about it," Penthesilea bowed, clapping the raving teenager on the shoulder in comfort. "Be strong, Kassandra. Protect your family from that horse you keep dreaming of."

The other Amazons were waiting at the steps of the palace as Penthesilea joined them.

"How are things in the palace?" her cousin Thermodossa inquired as they hastened towards the city's gates to resume the fight.

"Desperate—and in the town? Among the nobles, among the peasants?"

"Equally desperate. Today we'll need to fight as if our life depends on it—because it does."

"I agree. All but you, I have a special task for you. Take the shield from my back."

"Aye, lady." As she removed the shield from Penthesilea, she gasped in wonder. A slumbering child remained in the hollow of the shield, tied and secured to it by the handle.

"Whose is this?" she cried, shocked, but Penthesilea interrupted her.

"Take this child to the shepherds of Mount Ida. Raise him among them. No one can ever know whose child this is. His life depends upon it."

"You cannot steal the royal infant! You can be executed for it!"

"Andromache will never have me executed—she tied the boy to the shield with her own hand. This is the only way her child can be free, and she knows it. Take the rest of my gold and start a new life for him and yourself."

"But how will I smuggle him out of the city gates? What if he cries?"

"I fed him a few drops of poppy juice before I left. He will sleep the day. But you must reach Ida before nightfall."

"I—I cannot leave your side! I cannot abandon you to Achilles' wrath!"

"You must sacrifice your duty to protect this child. Please, Thermodossa, it's the only way. It's the only way I can protect the one I love. Will you do this for me? I can meet my fate with Achilles if I know you will do this for me."

Thermodossa, tears in her eyes, nodded in assent. "Aye." She saluted her queen and left.

Penthesilea strode out of the city gates and stopped. Looking up towards the ramparts, she gave a sad smile to the women who watched the battle from the walls and imagined that one of them was Andromache.

"You shall mourn over two tombs in Italy," she vowed, "but neither of them will be your son. Achilles may have taken your father, your brothers, your husband—he may take me, too—but your son shall be safe from his wrath."

With this last vow upon her lips, she lowered the helmet over her brow and strode into battle, ready to claim her destiny.

K.A. Masters is a fantasy writer who specializes in twisted fairy tales and zombie-infested historic fiction. She attributes her passion for Greco-Roma mythology and Germanic folklore to her alma mater, Dickinson College. Her debut novel, The Morning Tree, was published last year by Indie Gypsy.

The Encounter

By Sandy Dugger

The glow from the laptop illuminated Faith's face. Blue eyes squinted against the light before looking at the time once again. Nearly three in the morning and still no word from Erin, normally they would have already been chatting for hours, but with each minute that ticked away she feared she wouldn't be able to talk to her. Ten more minutes passed before she reached for the top of the laptop. The lid was almost shut when she heard the familiar ding. Light momentarily blinded her as she searched for the words from her girlfriend. Well, they had been calling each other that, but it would be another day before they actually would meet face to face.

Faith's heart pounded when she read the words, "Are you nervous?" Of course she was nervous. Six months ago when she started writing on a fan site about an Australian show, Moonshadow, she would have never thought she would find a girlfriend, much less one on the other side of the planet.

ERINFROMOZ: I'm not afraid to say I'm nervous.

Faith smiled before she typed her reply.

FAITH1984: Well then that makes me feel better. But I would say I'm more excited. I can't wait to feel you in my arms.

ERINFROMOZ: I know what you mean. The car can't get here fast enough. I'm afraid I forgot to pack something.

FAITH1984: If you do forget something we can get it after you arrive. I just want you here safe.

ERINFROMOZ: Oops got to go, the car's here. I'll text you before I get on the plane.

FAITH1984: Ok. I love you and I'll see you soon.

ERINFROMOZ: I love you too, bye. Sleep well.

Before Faith could reply she saw Erin sign off. Her heart was pounding. Even though she had to be up for work in less than four hours she didn't think she would be able to sleep. In a little over sixteen hours she would be able to hold Erin in her arms. Never had she imagined when she had started talking about her favorite character, Sara, on a fan site for some small Australian drama, that she would find the woman of her dreams. Erin had been the first person she really clicked with. Eventually Erin and Faith started chatting off the boards, and soon their friendship blossomed into something else.

Faith closed the lid to her laptop before she pushed it to the side of her bed. She curled up to dream about holding Erin in her arms. The only problem was she had no idea what Erin looked like. Even though Faith had sent a pic of herself to Erin, Erin had never sent one back. No amount of pleading could get Erin to send one. Every time she watched MTV's Catfish she hoped she wouldn't end up on that show someday. Her nervousness ended the day they finalized plans. But still Erin wouldn't send a photo. Instead she had told Faith what she would be wearing when she landed. It would have to be enough, plus Erin knew what Faith looked like. Faith's eyes drooped, and before she knew it Mr. Sandman had made his nightly visit.

"In six hours I'll be in your arms" was still posted on the screen.

The laptop was warm on Faith's lap. She had been looking at the screen for the past fifteen minutes reading those eight words repeatedly. Erin had long since signed off from her layover, and was now on the airplane half way to Portland. Her heart was racing at the thought that in just a few short hours she would finally see Erin. At last, Faith was no longer counting months or days, but hours and minutes.

She made one more sweep of her studio apartment making sure everything was in its place. The apartment had been cleaned the night before, but she still had a little time to waste before she headed to the airport. Reaching over she retrieved the latest list of items she would need for the weekend at the beach. Faith wanted to surprise Erin with a romantic weekend on the beach. She ran her finger down the list. She smiled as she reviewed each check mark indicating everything had been packed in the bags that lay beside the door. With a satisfied nod Faith closed the laptop and made her way to the bathroom to get ready to pick up Erin.

Faith casually leaned against a stone pillar as she waited for the passengers of Erin's flight to depart. She had been tracking the flight plan on her phone. The current information showed the plane had landed and the passengers were just starting to disembark. Her eyes scanned each person as they walked towards her. Faith was pulled back to her phone when she heard the familiar texting tone.

Erin: Just stepped off the plane and I'm on my way.
Faith: See you soon.
No reply came, so she returned to watching the

people pass by. Faith about dropped her phone when she saw who was walking towards her. She pressed her thumb to her iPhone and started to type.

Faith: OMG! I see Sara from Moonshadow. Did you see her on your flight?

Erin: Yes.

Faith: She is so beautiful. I mean she looks just like she does on the show.

Erin: Thank you.

Faith fumbled with the phone and barely caught it before it hit the ground. She felt heat start to creep up her neck. This couldn't be. Erin had to be playing a trick on her. Many nights she had heard herself laughing in her apartment about something Erin had said.

Faith: Haha, very funny.

Erin: I've been told I was quite cheeky when I was younger.

With her head still staring at her phone Faith spotted a pair of sneakers just in front of her. Slowly she raised her head. Her eyes were telling her brain that it was Sara standing in front of her, but she just couldn't believe it. It wasn't until the other woman spoke that she truly knew she had been telling Sara from Moonshadow she loved her.

"Hi," Erin said. The lopsided smile was the same one Sara had on her wallpaper on her laptop.

"Hi," Faith said. She knew she was going to be nervous meeting Erin, but now her anxieties was off the charts. How could it possibly be that the person she had been talking to, going on a year, was someone she watched on television?

They stood there not saying anything as seconds passed. A few more silent moments escaped before Erin finally said something.

"I'm sorry I didn't mean to deceive you, it's just…" The toe of her sneaker ground into the stained carpet.

"No, not at all. I mean I'm surprised, but really it's ok. I just, I mean. Wow. I can't believe it's you," Faith said. "Not, you as Sara, but just you. I mean the person I've been talking to for so long."

"It's me, it's always been me," Erin said.

When the shock finally wore off Faith reached out and pulled Erin into her arms. She felt Erin tense, then a moment later relax into her touch.

"I've been dreaming about this hug all day," Faith said.

"Me too." Erin's breath tickled Faith's neck causing a shiver to run down her spine.

Moments later they pulled away. Faith reached down and grabbed the bag Erin had dropped.

"How was your flight?" Faith asked as they made their way to baggage claim.

"Long, it's always a long flight when I come to the States."

"Are you tired?"

"Not really. I was able to nap on the plane." Silently they rode the elevator down. "So what do you have planned?"

"I was thinking we could get something to eat, it's going to be a few hours before we finally get out of the car."

"Food sounds heavenly, and I thought you lived in the city?" Erin's voice had taken on a breathy sound that caused Faith to blush.

"I do, but I actually have a surprise."

"Seems like I'm not the only one keeping secrets," Erin said, bumping Faith with her hip.

"I do have a few things planned."

"That sounds nice." The rest of the walk to luggage claim was spent talking about the flight.

As Erin pointed to her bags, Faith pulled them off the carousel. Silently they trudged through the garage. The summer in Portland was nearing triple digits, and with the humidity it was almost inhumane.

"Sorry about the heat, it's been unseasonably warm. Normally it's nice, but this summer has been brutal," Faith said as she started the car.

"It's ok, it will just keep us indoor most of the trip."

A blush started to creep up Faith's neck again. Erin laughed and before too long Faith's whole face was red.

"I didn't mean it like that," Erin said. She trailed a finger along Faith's hand that rested on the middle console, "but I wouldn't complain if that happened."

Faith concentrated on driving through the chaotic airport traffic as Erin continued to laugh.

"So, what would you like to eat?" Faith asked as she pulled onto the highway.

"Anything will beat what they serve on those flights."

"How about something fast that you can only find here, like Burgerville? It's on the way," Faith suggested.

Erin let out a moan that caused Faith's blush to flare up again.

"That sounds good, you've mentioned it a few times during our chats. I'm really looking forward to trying one of those cheeseburgers you keep raving about," Erin said.

"Ok, Burgerville it is then."

While they drove down the highway, every few seconds Faith would turn and glance at Erin.

"What?"

"What, what?" Faith said.

"You keep staring, do I have something on my face," Erin flipped down the visor, but there was no mirror.

"No, I'm sorry. I just can't believe it's you. I mean, I can't believe you're here, I'll admit that for a few minutes I thought I was being catfished, or trolled by some old dude just having fun?" Faith said before taking another glance at her passenger.

"I'm sorry. Are you upset that I didn't tell you who I was?" Erin shifted in her seat so she could look at Faith.

"Upset, no, I'm surprised. But the fact that you're Taylor Richter is a bit of a shocker. I won't lie." Faith chanced another glance.

"I'm sorry I deceived you. I've had this problem meeting people before. It's hard for people to see me for me and not the actress."

"But what do I call you? I mean is Taylor your name or Erin?"

"Erin is fine. Erin is my middle name. Taylor is my first name, but all my true friends call me Erin."

Faith smiled and took another glance.

"I like that. I mean the friend part."

Erin placed her hand over Faith's. She squeezed till Faith faced her.

"I like to think we are more than just friends."

"Good, me too, I didn't want to overstep my bounds." Faith said.

"You could walk for miles and not overstep." Erin again squeezed Faith's hand before she released it.

Faith didn't know how to reply, but before Erin could totally remove her hand, Faith grabbed it and held it until they pulled into the Burgerville parking lot.

When they entered Faith found a booth and Erin ordered. As Faith sat down with their meal Faith noticed whispers and a few long glances.

"Does this happen to you everywhere you go?" Faith asked as she nodded to the couple next to them who suspiciously had their cell phones pointed in their direction.

"Back home, yes, when I'm in the States, not so much," Erin said as she bit into her cheeseburger. Some of the sauces dripped onto her fingers. With rapt attention Faith watched Erin suck the yellowish liquid from her fingers.

"Oh my god, this is so good." Erin said.

Another blush spread across Faith's cheeks. For the rest of the meal she tried to keep her eyes on her own tray. As they exited she bought a bottle of the cheeseburger spread.

Safely back on the road Faith glanced at Erin, "I'm sorry, but I'm curious. Why didn't you tell me who you were earlier?"

"I'm sorry, I didn't mean to deceive you. It's just that in the past, when I've tried dating, I've gotten the feeling that people don't want to be with me, but with Taylor the movie star."

Faith nodded as she continued to watch the road.

"The internet was my way to be free, to be me. I didn't have to put on a show or smile for the camera. It allowed me to be who I really am. Talking to you every day was the highlight of my day. It was something I looked forward to. I found someone who wanted me for me, not for the person they saw on the screen or in the magazines," Erin said, her finger rhythmically locking and unlocking the car door.

Faith focused on the highway said, "I understand." She stole a glance at Erin. The only thing she could see was the back of her head.

"I want you to know I fell in love with you, not the person on the screen. Your words were what drew me to you. The way you were so honest and open. You answered every question and allowed me to be me too. I sometimes feel like when you meet someone you have to try to impress them. With you it felt great to be me, and not have to think if I was saying the right thing."

"I'm glad. I know what you mean. It was refreshing to just put everything out there. It was almost like I was hiding behind the screen, but the truth was, I was more honest with you then I have ever been with anybody else. I loved every time we chatted. I didn't have to watch my every word, it was wonderful not having to think about what I said, wonder if it was going to come back and bite me sometime in the future."

"Don't worry, I don't bite," Faith said.

"That's a bummer," Erin whispered. The words hung in the car like a mist. A few seconds passed before both women broke into uncontrollable laughter.

A minute passed before Faith could respond.

"Well if you're into that sort of thing. I might be willing to have a nibble or two."

"I'm looking forward to it." Another laugh burst from Erin as Faith focused on the road. "You're just so cute. You blush at everything."

"I know, I hate it," Faith pouted. She could even feel her ears burning.

"I find it adorable," Erin said before she squeezed

Faith's leg. Faith flinched at the touch. When Erin started to pull back, Faith placed her hand on Erin's to keep it where it was.

The drive along the highway was exquisite torture as Faith tried to hold it together. The feeling of Erin's hand on her thigh was driving her insane. She pushed the speed limit as much as she could as she passed cars on the winding road through the coastal mountains. Erin's hand had started a dizzying path from her knee that slowly came closer and closer to Faiths center.

Almost two hours on the road passed before Faith pulled into the driveway of her parent's beach home. She put the car in park and let out a sigh.

"We're here," Faith said before she exited the car. The salty air and sound of waves crashing on the beach welcomed her. The sun was just starting to set in the west.

"The bags can wait." Faith held out her hand and Erin slipped hers into it. Silently they walked around the back and down the steep embankment. The sand shifted under their feet as they made their way along the beach. Faith directed Erin to a huge log a few steps away. Both women sat down. With their fingers still entwined they watched the sun paint the sky with dazzling colors of blue, pink, orange and red.

It was getting late, and as the fog started to roll in so did the chilly evening air. Nothing was said as the two women made their way back to the house.

Faith retrieved the bags and shouldered the door.

"Make yourself at home," Faith said before hefting the bags upstairs.

A few minutes later Faith returned and settled into the couch, at the opposite end from where Erin was sitting.

"You can sit closer," Erin said with a mischievous grin.

Moving closer, Faith felt more relaxed, now that the flirty Erin was back. It was like over the phone or online. Erin patted her lap, and Faith laid her head down. Faith nestled into her. She felt strong fingers thread their way through her hair.

"It's just as silky as I imagined it would be." Faith heard her say, still continuing to run her fingers through her hair.

"Thank you," Faith said before trailing her own finger across Erin's knee. She could feel shocks ripple through her.

"I'm glad I'm here with you."

"So am I," Faith said moving her hand further up Erin's leg. "Is this okay?"

Erin's "yes" came out like a hiss.

"If we want to do anything today, you may want to stop what you are doing or we won't be going anywhere else tonight," Erin said.

Faith gazed into piercing blue eyes. Her heart started to race as she saw desire staring back at her. "I think," Faith said as she reached up to cup Erin's cheek, "I want to stay in."

Faith rose so their lips met for a searing kiss. She tried to fill the kiss with all the passion that had been building for months.

Erin pulled back after a few moments, her eyes never leaving Faith's.

"Are you sure this is what you want?"

"If you're asking me if I'm sure if I want to go upstairs and do what we've talked about online? I want that now, more than I want to breathe." Faith didn't know where that came from, but once it was out of her mouth she knew it was the truth.

Faith sat up and swung her legs off the couch. She held out a hand waiting for Erin to take it. Her nerve began to waver the longer she stood waiting. Faith was moments away from telling Erin they didn't have to go upstairs when Erin stood and took her hand.

It felt like Faith was floating as they walked up the stairs. The bedroom door was open. Their eyes locked as Faith started removing her clothes. As each article of clothing was removed they were tossed into the lone chair in the corner. Erin's eyes never left the body that was being unwrapped for her. Finally naked, Faith sat on the edge of the bed. With each passing second she began to feel exposed. Normally, she would have wrapped her arms around her body to try and cover up, but she wanted to express to Erin that she wanted this. To relay silently that she was sure of what was about to happen.

Still standing in the doorway, Erin slowly started to remove her own clothes, allowing Faith to take in every piece of uncovered flesh. Her body was perfection. Not perfect in the fact that she was muscular or lithe, Erin's body was real with curves that Faith longed to caress. Erin slowly walked over to Faith leaving her clothes where they had fallen. Faith had seen Erin's body exposed on television, but the screen did not do her body justice.

"I know we've talked about personal details online, but now that I'm here, and you know I'm real, I need to know, do you trust me?" Erin's words caressed Faith's skin like silk.

"Yes," Faith whispered, unable to hold back the goose bumps that now covered her body. She could hear the sound of the waves crashing against the beach through the open window, a sound that was soon drowned out by the pounding of her heart.

"Good, I want you to lie back." Faith did as Erin instructed. Erin slowly climbed onto the bed and straddled her abdomen.

"If at any time you feel scared or uncomfortable say table and I'll stop. Do you understand?" Faith nodded. "Good."

Erin hopped off the bed and went to her luggage. With a few things in her hands she sauntered back to the bed. Faith's eyes never left Erin's body. With the grace of a dancer Erin made her way back to the bed. Heat from her center spread across Faith's belly as Erin returned to her earlier spot.

She brought Faith's right hand to her lips kissing each finger. Erin separated the silk scarves. She tied the end of one of the scarves around Faith's wrist. Faith felt a twinge of fear, but the excitement of what was happening was stronger. Her lover tied the other end around the bedpost leaving her arms enough room to move. The same thing was duplicated with her other arm. The scarves were not tight and Faith knew if she really wanted to get out it was possible.

Erin slid down Faith's body until it rested the entire length of her lover's. Full lips hovered next to Faith. She couldn't suppress another moan when their lips met again moving as one. Faith's overheated body started writhing against Erin.

Butterfly kisses were placed on Faith's cheek as she made her way down her body. Faith strained against the scarves as she longed to run her hands through Erin's hair to show her where she needed her lips to be. Arching her back, she offered up both her breasts to Erin's eager mouth.

When her tongue flicked over Faith's hardened nipple, it felt as if a bolt of lightening ran through both her breasts ending at her pussy. Her body was alive with desire and Erin's tongue was slowly igniting a bonfire.

The wetness between her legs continued to grow as Erin nipped and licked her breasts. Faith's hips bucked trying to connect to relieve the pressure between her legs that her bound hands yearned to touch. Faith wrapped her legs around Erin's waist. Stronger hands pried Faith's legs apart.

Erin rolled off Faith, severing all contact. A moan of frustration filled the silence. Strong hands caressed Faith's legs from her knee to her silky wet folds. She moaned when she felt Erin's hand brush against her sensitive lips. Spreading her legs, she silently begged for Erin's touch. Faith wanted release in the worst way. Again, she tried to move her hands to ease the tension that only her fingers knew how to release, but again the scarves stopped her. Her hips bucked as she felt a lone finger slip between her swollen lips.

Faith needed Erin to stroke her aching clit, but when two fingers found their way to her slippery entrance she moaned in pleasure. Slowly Erin stroked her velvety walls curving her fingers. Faith rocked her hips, setting the pace. Strong hands pumped in and out matching her speed. Soon Erin added a third finger. Through their many conversations Erin knew Faith's desire to be taken hard. Long moments passed before Erin removed her fingers and focused her attention on Faith's aching clit. Fingers slowly stroked Faith's clit from top to bottom. Her hips started grinding in a circular motion trying to add pressure, directing Erin's fingers to where she needed her most.

"Harder," Faith begged. "Please, I'm so close." Her body rocked against Erin's hand as she rubbed her hard bundle of nerves.

Faith grabbed the scarves pulling them tight against the headboard as she barreled down on Erin's skillful fingers. "Oh God, I'm close."

Erin's lips were at her ear nipping and sucking her sensitive lobe. Soft whispers penetrated the fog of desire she had wrapped around her. "Come for me," turned into a mantra that sent Faith over the edge.

"Oh God I'm coming," Faith shouted as her orgasm crashed over her. Erin's fingers continued to stroke her clit.

Faith melted back into the bed, chest heaving, trying to slow her breathing. Erin knelt by her head, swift fingers untying her wrists. Erin started to move, when a strong hand reached out and stilled her body.

"No don't move," Faith said, before sitting up.

Rubbing her wrists she attempted to get the circulation flowing again. She didn't want them to be cold when she placed them on Erin's warm body. From behind Faith spread her legs while kissing Erin's soft shoulders. She ran her hands up her body caressing Erin's supple skin. Cupping her breasts she caressed them as she ground her hips into her ass.

Faith removed her hands, backing up, "move over a bit, more to the center," She told her.

Erin moved to the center of the bed. Faith placed her hands on top of Erin's and placed them on top of the headboard. Sliding her hands over her bare arms, she made a trail to her bare ass.

"Sit up a bit," Faith told her as she rubbed her supple cheeks.

She did as Faith asked, raising her hips up. Faith

lay down on her back and slid under Erin. Wrapping her arms around powerful thighs, she pulled Erin down toward her hungry mouth.

Erins' center sat above Faith, stretched open by her spread legs. Faith wrapped her arms around Erin's thighs before she pulled her center down toward her hungry mouth. Faith ran her tongue along Erin's wet folds until she entered her. Her needy tongue attempted to lick every drop that she had. Soft moans and whimpers escaped Erin's lips as her hips rode Faith's tongue.

Faith kissed Erin's pulsing bundle of nerves. Licking and nipping, she tried to match her hips stroke for stroke, letting her set the pace. Erin continued to buck as her breath came quicker. Her legs started to shake against the side of Faith's head. Erin was close… she was so very close that Faith could feel it. Seconds later Erin's scream pierced the air.

Faith's eyes snapped open as the blaring music began to penetrate her sleeping brain. She turned the alarm off and tried to recapture the dream that had plagued her for months. The clock's time displayed that she only had another four hours until she would be heading to the airport to pick up the woman she had been talking to over the internet. With a sigh Faith tossed the blankets off her and prepared to meet the woman she had been in love with for months.

Sandy Dugger spends her days in Maricopa Arizona fielding tech questions during the day and writing stories at night. When she isn't working she is spending as much time with friends, family, and her dog Tara. She tries to get out as much as possible with her RV'ing group RVW.

Who's Afraid of the Pink Fairy?

By Gabriela Martins

The first time Lina saw the pink girl she was five. She wasn't scared, but then again, not many things that were real scared a five-year-old.

It was past Lina's bedtime, but she wasn't sleeping. She kept the window open, and stared at the stars, as she counted sheep with her eyes open. Her blanket, long forgotten, pooled around her legs as she sat cross-legged in front of the window, watching, like she knew deep down that something special was about to happen.

She didn't understand at first, when the air became thicker and she felt shivers up her spine. She frowned in confusion, and it took her eyes a second to adjust to the sudden neon lights that came from Tania's hair.

Tania stood, not much taller than her, suspended in air. The child fairy was a bit older than Lina, but her hair was considerably longer, cascading down her back and torso and past her hips. It was pink, sometimes bright and shiny, and fading to purple. Her skin was a pale tone of brown. Her eyebrows were made of glitter, and her eyes a sparkly blue that seemed to slit as she blinked curiously at Lina. Tania's mouth was tinted rose and she was wearing a white gown. Lina's lips parted, but no voice came just yet. Tania stared at her, and Lina stared right back.

"Who are you?" she asked, when she found her voice.

Tania tilted her head to the side. "Tania," she replied, like it was a silly question.

If Lina had been older, perhaps she'd know to ask Tania where she came from, but she wasn't, and therefore she didn't. She wasn't scared of Tania's suddenness or of her odd looks. All she knew was that she had a new friend to play with, one that could appear and disappear at will.

The next day, when she told her parents, they dismissed it with fond smiles, giggling to themselves that Lina had created an imaginary friend so she wouldn't be alone.

⁂

"I envy you," Lina said with a scowl, dropping heavily on the bed. Because that didn't cause Tania to show herself, Lina added, staring at the ceiling "I know you're here, Tania."

There was a smile on the corner of her lips as she said this, and the next thing she heard was Tania's soft laughter. She pulled herself to her elbows, watching as Tania quietly entered her room through the window, pulling her massive hair to her front. She smirked, and Tania smirked back.

"And why is that, Lina?" Tania asked, using a tone that sounded like she was just humoring Lina.

Tania didn't believe in envy. She liked to claim that human emotions were like beliefs, just as easily as you could believe they existed…you could also dismiss them as entirely illusionary. Tania used words like illusionary.

"For starters, you don't need to go to school, so you never had to take any exams—"

"Fairies are tested in different ways," Tania interrupted.

Lina continued as if there'd been no interruptions.

"Plus, you don't need to deal with anyone's drama if you don't want to. There's this guy in my Spanish class, Billy, and he's freaking out because of his thirteenth birthday. How weird is that?"

Tania regarded her with a small smile for a second, and without reason, Lina blushed. That had been happening more often than not these days.

Looking down, she suddenly felt conscious of her gray pajamas and her Mickey Mouse socks. She chewed on her bottom lip, and stared down at her thighs.

She'd seen Tania outside of her room, but only a few times. Usually, they met in Lina's room, where nobody could interrupt their endless conversations, about human literature and the stars and fairies' long expansive wings that only arrived after a certain age. They'd share concerns about feeling at ease in their own skin, or not at all. Lina didn't understand what it was like for Tania, being the youngest of fifteen sisters, expected to outshine at the very least half of them, with her magic and prodigy. Tania couldn't possibly understand what it was like for Lina, with her divorced parents and the promise of high school around the corner. They did their best to nod along. When other barriers arose in their friendship, they just kept nodding along.

❧ ❧ ❧

Outside of her room, it'd be dangerous. Two

years ago, when Lina was eleven—Tania had given her a necklace. It was a magical beautiful thing. When Lina traveled to Guadalajara in Mexico to see family, she'd used the necklace to call for her best friend, and hoped Tania could make herself invisible to the others. She couldn't. A cousin saw Tania's long bright pink hair, and for a moment, they'd both held their breath. Lina's cousin had also been drinking, and disappointed in himself for seeing things, he'd just gone to bed early.

"I was just thinking about how strange things can be," Tania said, walking to the end of Lina's bed and sitting down. Lina came a little closer, like Tania was a magnet. "You know the first time I came here—"

"It was an accident. You were looking for one of your sisters, but calculated the directions wrong."

Tania slapped the mattress and made a funny face. "Let me finish, Lina!" she laughed, and Lina laughed too, apologizing and nodding.

"But yes, it was. I thought I'd find Mianee, but I found you instead," she paused, cocking a glittery eyebrow that shone in pearl, gold, and silver. "My human friend."

Lina smirked, dimples piercing her cheeks. Her chest inflated with pride. "That's cool, isn't it? I'm your secret. You're mine."

Lina felt like giggling, while repeating the words out loud, "you're mine." These words reminded Lina of her older brother who was obsessed with heart-shaped sweets that had printed words on them like, be mine.

"Oh, to imagine the elders' faces if they knew I had a human friend," Tania entertained the idea, with a vague smile lingering on her lips. "That would be… imprudent."

Lina smiled. She liked that.

Pulling herself even closer to Tania, she touched the fairy's hands to her own, bringing Tania's brown hands with perfectly manicured pink nails to her lap.

"Tell me about your day! What did you do?" But Tania disappeared.

⚜ ⚜ ⚜ ⚜

Lina had been biting her nails chewing the skin around her fingernails and ruining the black nail polish. Every extended family dinner that seemed to never end only made her more nervous, causing her leg to bounce up and down. Her mother called her on it, but in that moment her brother tried to bring attention back to him, and as they spiraled into yet another fight, Lina was finally excused to go to her room.

Lina practically slammed the door of her room as she entered hoping the sound would call Tania, but still nothing happened. She swallowed dryly, her hands close to shaking, and rushed to the window, opening it widely. It was a starless night, cloudy and heavy and carrying the smell of approaching rain.

Lina pressed her lips together, looking up, but still saw nothing. Her lips quivered, and she turned away from the window, practically running as she fell down on her knees just next to her bed. She pulled a music box from under the bed, ignoring dirty clothes and other neglected boxes. Inside, there were a few pairs of earrings and bracelets her mother had tried to get her to wear, but that wasn't what she was looking for. It was the necklace Tania gave her.

She took a deep breath, bringing the necklace close to her heart, and closed her eyes. She felt the warmth that came from the stone that touched her skin, and very softly, she whispered "Please, Tania, please come and find me. I...I need you."

When she pulled the necklace away from her chest, her vision was blurry. She took a deep breath and put the jewelry box back under her bed. Still on the floor, she let her head fall, her chin hitting the spot between her shoulders while shutting her eyes tight. Her hands went to the torn fabric in her black jeans, where she could touch her own skin, and just press it to feel that she was real.

She was real. She existed. Just like Tania did too. In two different worlds, they existed, and this bedroom was their gray area—the only place they could both exist at once.

"You called."

She turned around, and there she was. Reliable, beautiful Tania, with her long pink wings that had come not long ago, in the week Lina had turned seventeen. She was wearing a dark purple and green dress that seemed to shine as she moved, her long legs showing as she walked quietly to the center of the room, barefoot.

Lina felt something tighten in her chest, and she went up to Tania, throwing her arms around her. She was a volcano about to erupt, but it was all right, because she wasn't alone. Her best friend was there to catch her, arms going around her middle, protective wings circling them both in an impenetrable bubble.

She kept her eyes closed, but she somehow knew Tania's were closed too.

"She hates me," Lina said in a whisper, her face pressed against Tania's warm shoulder. "She just hates me. She can't look me in the eye anymore."

Tania's fingers slid up and down her back to soothe her, and her voice sounded like a dream when she said, "Your mom will come around. It's what mothers do."

Not always, Lina wanted to say. It's not always what mothers do.

"In no time, she'll be glad you told the truth about who you are." Tania said.

Lina wasn't sure—wasn't ever sure when it came to her parents. She nodded, putting distance between them slowly, and then pausing and coming closer to Tania until there were only a few inches between them again. She sniffed, wiping the tears off her face with the back of her hand and a small smile, and watched Tania's lips shape into a smile as well, her wings retracting until they became long slits on Tania's back.

"I didn't want to lie anymore," she added, as an afterthought.

Tania didn't take a step back like the girls at school would've when Lina was speaking quietly about whom she was. Tania just frowned slightly.

"I don't even understand why that counts as lying. Why would your Mom have assumed you were heterosexual before? She never asked, did she?"

Laughing quietly, Lina lifted her shoulders. "You have a point, fairy girl. I guess fairies are smarter than humans."

With a smirk, Tania cocked an eyebrow. "I've been saying this since you were five, Lina. Only now you are catching up? I wonder if it's because my kind's smarter…"

"Hey!" Lina made a face and fake punched Tania's shoulder.

Tania laughed and Lina laughed, and for a little while, it didn't feel as strange to be in this house she'd lived in her whole life. Because of Tania, her room was a safe haven.

Much later, when they both were lying on Lina's bed, Tania had her head on Lina's lap and Lina had her hands on the endless mane of pink that was Tania's hair, Lina found herself asking about Tania's recent training. All she'd known was that Tania had been meeting with the fairies that circled the sea and the ice, getting stronger and ready for battles that Lina's humankind would never take part in or even acknowledge.

"It's a tense time for us," Tania said, closing her eyes softly. Even her eyelashes, thin and long, looked made of gold. "It may be a while before I come back. I don't know how long. Mother wants me and my sisters to spend some time north, training for the next big battle."

Lina nodded, feeling her throat close, and her eyes tear up.

She was silent for heaven knows how long, but her stomach still dropped as if she'd just been caught off guard. When Tania opened her eyes again, and with a concerned frown, asked, "What's wrong, Leen?"

Lina tried to smile, but it felt forced. "I don't want you to get hurt in those stupid wars."

She assumed Tania's odd expression was her way of trying to smile back, but it didn't feel any more sincere than Lina's forced smile had.

Tania pulled herself up to sit, and with her outer thigh pressing against Lina's, she touched the side of her face.

"Don't worry, my human friend," she smirked up, and this time it seemed like a genuine smile. Lina held her breath, and tilted her chin up just slightly, locking eyes with Tania.

"It's going to be alright. When I come back, I'll

be more than a fairy," she paused, her thumb circling Lina's chin. "I'll be a warrior."

Lina laughed quietly and then felt sad at the notion. She held back tears and breathed out in a rush. "I think I'd prefer you alive."

"I'll be alive, alright. It's a promise."

But as she said it, Tania dropped her hand from Lina's face, and it didn't feel like a promise anymore. Lina took a deep breath, her arms going around Tania's neck and she closed her eyes as she hugged Tania close…so close that she felt Tania's heart beating against hers.

"I'll miss you, Leen," Tania whispered in her ear.

Lina could feel her breath close, her mouth still lingering nearby, and she wondered, for a split second, if Tania knew what it did to her to be that close to each other.

Instead of questioning that, she tried to gather the courage to look Tania in the eye again. Letting her go, hands sliding down Tania's shoulders, she looked into her otherworldly eyes again.

"When you come back…I'll probably be in college."

They'd talked about this many times.

It hadn't been easy the first, or second, or third time they discussed it.

A shadow passed Tania's face, but like they always did, she nodded. She tried to smile and Lina didn't. Lina's hand reached Tania's, and with their fingers enlaced, she stared at the contrast of their skin and nails and how it mattered little, even though they weren't made of the same blood or energy.

"I'll have a roommate," Lina recited the words she knew by heart, "we can't meet then. It's too dangerous.

If anyone else sees you…it'd be dangerous. It would be bad for you."

"It would." Tania agreed, her thumb caressing Lina's as her eyes looked down as well. "It would be very bad indeed."

"But—" Lina choked up.

Tania smiled at her sideways like she understood. It was enough encouragement to try again.

"But I don't know if I can do this without you." Lina said.

This time, Tania didn't smile. She looked down and her long eyelashes were a distraction to the whirlwind in Lina's mind. She pressed her fingers to her plump pink lips and sighed. She never asked why Lina couldn't do without her, or what the future would hold for them. Instead, she nodded.

"Do you believe in missing people?" Lina asked, with a little laugh, when Tania met her eyes. "Missing them like you'd miss a limb. Just—really bad."

Tania cocked a glittery eyebrow, and considered this. "I think I'm about to find out just how legitimate this human emotion is."

Lina licked her lips, looking at Tania then. She never wanted to kiss anyone as badly as she wanted to kiss the pink fairy that had entered her life by mistake.

But soon there was a war on the one side, and college on the other, and between those, there wouldn't be much she could do to keep up with the emotions spiraling out of control inside her.

So she sank her teeth onto her bottom lip, and smiled.

It came out broken, but Tania smiled back, mirroring her.

❧❧❧❧

Midterms were hell, Lina was convinced, but hell was a concept that bended and changed shape, depending on what mood she was in. First semester of college was difficult, because Lina didn't like most of her professors, didn't understand about half of what she learned in class, and there were no good friends around. Mostly, though, she missed Tania.

Lina's fingers drummed against her notebook, notes about Algebra getting scrambled with song lyrics, and she absentmindedly regarded her professor, as the woman paced around the stage, lecturing them on things that would hardly be useful in four years. In her backpack, she carried the necklace.

She didn't know why she brought it everywhere, really. It wasn't like she could just summon Tania. She knew that even if she did find a quiet place where they wouldn't be bothered, Tania was way up north, close to the sea, fighting wars that she had no business wondering about.

Still she wondered.

It was a lie she told herself, though…she did know exactly why she brought the necklace with her everywhere. She knew that one day, she just wouldn't be able to take missing Tania anymore, and she'd call her. Winter break couldn't come fast enough.

❧❧❧❧

Her mother seemed so preoccupied with her brother that, for once, the spotlight wasn't on her. Her brother had been caught smoking weed in the school parking lot, and her mother was going on and on about how this was all her father's fault, while grandma pretended the fight wasn't happening, and held Lina's hands asking her a million questions about college.

Lina tried to answer them as truthfully as she could, doing her best to ignore the arguing as her brother flipped their mother off, and her mom started yelling at him.

"Grandma, I'm not feeling well," Lina said, which wasn't a complete lie. "Would you tell Mom I went upstairs for a nap before dinner?"

Grandma smiled. "Sure thing, dear. You must be tired. Traveling all the way back home...I wasn't sure you'd like to come home," she squeezed Lina's hand, her tone of voice growing resigned.

Lina wanted to sigh, but instead she lifted her shoulders, as a small vacant smile came across her lips.

"Go," grandma said, "go to your room, dear. I'll tell them."

She went up, two steps at a time, and when she reached her room, she nearly cried. Lina opened the window wide, and with a feeling like her heart was climbing up into her throat, she unpacked the necklace from around the velvet that wrapped it, and brought it close to her chest.

With her eyes closed, she said a little prayer before she called for Tania. Her door was locked, and the night breeze washed all the anxiety away.

"Missed me?"

She opened her eyes, and right in front of her, with her wings spread wide outside her window, Tania stood tall, with her chin tilted up, and a scar that cut her brown skin from just under her eye all the way down to her chin. It'd scarred well, and she looked bright. Her glittery eyebrows only made her eyes bigger and brighter, and her hair cascaded, like it always did, in pink and rose and curled around the ends.

Lina let go of the necklace, choked up, and took a step back so Tania could come in. The corner of Tania's mouth went up in a smile, and the second her bare feet touched the dark green carpet, Lina launched herself at her, smiling so widely that she thought her face might split.

Tania giggled quietly, holding her so tight that Lina couldn't take it. She pulled away, not enough that they separated, but enough that they could look each other in the eye.

"I did. I did miss you lots and lots." Lina said.

Tania smirked up at her, hands still on her waistline, and Lina knew, without a doubt, that there was no next logical step other than the one she was taking. She held the side of Tania's beautiful face, and they locked eyes until their foreheads touched. Lina was still smiling, and Tania was still smiling, but their eyes closed when their lips got closer.

Lina covered Tania's lips with hers, and though she was sure her chest would explode, it didn't.

For the first time, in a long time, she wasn't scared.

Then again, not many things scared a woman in love.

Gabriela Martins is a Brazilian author with terrifying obsessions with witches, fictional wars and superheros. Her main hobbies include plotting murders to happen within made up worlds, long walks to the couch to binge-watch TV shows on Netflix, and surprisingly, Yoga.

Perchance to Dream

By Lea Daley

For anyone keeping score, my long-range romance began with a white lie. The recipient of my impulsive deception was Bette Hinson—*Bête Noire*, as I called her privately—a pretty and pretty self-satisfied colleague, who'd been an irritant from day one. Whenever possible, I tuned her out. She not only saw herself as the center of the universe and our office social director, but as a sublimely superior specimen of all things lesbian.

In a heightened voice, with obvious intent to embarrass me, she asked, "Why not bring a date to the Valentine's party on Friday?"

Why not? I thought. *Because I was terminally single, that's why. I'd yet to find the woman who swooned in the presence of my imposing height, hung on my every opinionated word, or shared my passion for Europe. But no way was I offering her that information.*

"That's not possible, Bette," I said breezily. "My fiancée is in France."

She looked at me with the first hint of interest. I'd watched her blue eyes widen, then sweep the length of my body.

"You have a girlfriend? How did I not know? And when will she return?"

"Maybe never," I said, winging it, enjoying messing with her. "She renewed her visa a while back, but she's not sure she wants to visit the U.S., given our current political climate."

Bette leaned across her desk, unmistakably intrigued, exposing lush cleavage for my inspection.

"She was born there? She's actually French?"

"With a name like Delphine Sauvage, what else would she be?"

Bette dropped back into her chair and crossed her arms.

"Spill, Val. Every…single…thing."

"Can't," I said, flicking off my monitor. "I'm late for an appointment."

Before I reached the exit, the beast called out, "Let's pick this up tomorrow. Over lunch."

Imagine that, lunch with Bette. A first. It could be fun to spin out my tantalizing little fiancée fantasy for her, but I'd need to invent a lot of juicy details before then. Turning back, I waved.

"Tomorrow, then," I said.

The appointment I'd mentioned was with Kamikazi, my exuberant Airedale terrier, a deluxe pizza, and my TV. As soon as I'd given Kami a well-deserved run and paid the delivery dude, I settled in front of the final season of *The Americans*. As much as I loved the series—as relevant as it seemed now with Trump in the Oval Office—I couldn't concentrate on the enticing, ever-changing actress Keri Russell. And that was Delphine's fault—the ravishing, desirable, imaginary Delphine. Having conjured up such an intriguing phantom, I couldn't quit thinking about her. After muting my flat screen, I closed my eyes.

What did she look like?

The image rose up instantly, rushed through me. My idea of the ultimate French beauty—a bit femme, but proud, strong—dark hair cut in a mussed elfin style that was probably long out of date, since my last trip to Paris was several years ago. Expressive, burnt umber colored eyes, long and narrow, with lashes so naturally lush the fashion police might cite her for indiscriminate use of mascara. High cheekbones, a wide, welcoming smile... slender, and shorter than I—wasn't everybody?—but not by much. She'd tan without trying, and, unlike me, would be totally at ease on the topless beaches of the Riviera.

What would she be doing just then? Given the six-hour time difference between us, probably getting ready for bed. But before that she might be walking a fluffy dog, just the right size for a cozy little apartment. She'd have a confident, uninhibited stride that chewed up urban sidewalks as if she owned the world. And since it was a weeknight, she'd have eaten in her favorite restaurant. I'd long ago learned that Parisians mostly dine out, cooking at home only on weekends. After dinner, she'd have waited for me to get off work so we could spend a precious few hours on FaceTime or Skype. Skype naturally being our preferred mode, given its greater suitability for sex play—

Something heavy struck the floor overhead, jolting me from my reverie. The upstairs neighbor had arrived. Blinking, I looked around. My tidy, boring, living room seemed hazy, unreal—my actual life, likewise. Kami stretched and began to lick my hand rhythmically, but it wasn't especially comforting.

I suddenly ached for Delphine. Whose signature scent seemed to linger in the air.

Shaking off the fantasy, laughing at how real it

felt, I pushed myself through my evening routine. On the way to bed, I grabbed a tablet and pen, with no clear purpose in mind. But once I was propped against my pillows, with Kami curled at my feet, I began to write…

Ma chère Delphine,

No one has understood me as you do, loved me so unconditionally, and trusted me so completely. Our next meeting seems impossibly far away. I long for the moment of reunion, when it's possible to touch you once more. When being touched is like being ushered into heaven…

The tablet fell to the duvet, my thighs fell open, and surely that must be Delphine's hand seeking the sweet spot, because nothing had ever felt so glorious, so perfectly attuned to my needs, so capable of taking me to new heights… And as I drifted off, perhaps it was only my blankets gathered in a mound behind me, but I thought Delphine's warm body was pressed against the length of mine.

My alarm not only woke me, it shattered that foolish fiction. As I staggered toward the coffeemaker, I snorted at the idea that so magnificent a creature could love me.

"In your dreams," I said aloud. "Literally."

Because it had been a dream, no matter how concrete it felt. Still, in the shower, a huge smile kept washing over my face as I revisited Delphine's touch, recreated it once more, rinse and repeat…

At work, I was so focused on completing a grant proposal that all thoughts of the fantasy fled. Yet my subconscious must have been hard at work behind the scenes, fleshing out my mysterious lover. During lunch with Bette, Delphine's personality seemed so well defined she might as well have been flipping through the standard American menu, wrinkling her aristocratic nose at garish photos of salads and burgers, her continental suspicion on full display. And under Bette's relentless probing, my imaginary history with Delphine unreeled effortlessly.

We'd met five years earlier. When I made reservations to stay at an ancient hotel in the heart of Paris, I never guessed love would find me in a courtyard there. Our paths had crossed during the magic hour, seemingly by chance. But luxuriating in that golden light, nearly overcome by the fragrance of lavender and lemon balm, perhaps I'd noticed an intriguing woman gazing down from a wrought iron balcony. And perhaps she'd dashed outdoors to introduce herself. Maybe we fell into conversation—me in halting high school French, she in more proficient English, albeit with a spellbinding accent. Perhaps we'd each found something deeply satisfying in the other's gaze...

A severely edited version of those scenes was all I intended to disclose to Bette. But she wasn't easily put off. As she probed, I invented more and more of Delphine's world, so involved in the challenge that I barely touched my salad.

"My weeklong stay at the hotel became two, then three," I said. "To be near her, I sacrificed a visit to Venice, then a trip to Rome. She's a film editor. Mostly documentaries. She hopes to direct one day."

"And she lives in Paris?"

"On the Île St. Louis. Do you know it?"

"I've never left the States. I really don't see the point."

I smiled fondly. "The Île is a pricey plot of land in the middle of the Seine. As it happens, Delphine's family owns the inn where I stayed on my first visit to France. The island is charming—very small, but filled with majestic old homes. The streets are lined with luxury boutiques, cafés, and bakeries. Recently trendier shops have displaced some of the older enterprises, but it's still one of my favorite places."

"So Delphine never visits you?" The hint of skepticism in Bette's voice told me she'd been asking around, to no avail. Because while several coworkers were aware of my addiction to travel, no one could have known anything about a long distance love affair.

Reaching for the check, I managed to laugh. "She did in the beginning. But I'd much rather spend my vacation time in Europe, seeing new sights with her."

"Too bad," Bette said. "I'd like to meet her."

"Highly unlikely. Are you ready to go?"

That afternoon, work was a bear. I should have been exhausted by the time I unlocked my front door. Instead, as soon as the demands of the day faded from conscious thought, the idea of Delphine rushed in. I took Kami for a walk, yet hardly noticed the winding paths of Central Park, the street musicians, and the mimes. Back at home, while heating a frozen dinner, I cooked up a delicious new interlude in Paris...

We'd talked for an hour in that courtyard, scarcely pausing for breath. Then Delphine had canted a narrow wrist to glance at her watch.

"As much as I have enjoyed our conversation, I must go. Our cook's husband is ill and I have promised to prepare many quiches for tomorrow's breakfast..."

The thought of parting was almost physically painful. "Perhaps I could help...?"

"Do you cook?"

I winced. "Not really. But I can take direction."

Delphine's dark eyes met mine, sparkling wickedly as she considered an unintended subtext. "That sounds promising." Pulling me upright, she said, "Come."

"Right here?" I quipped, not sure whether the joke would translate—or if I'd crossed a line. But her low laugh assured me we were of one mind.

The hotel kitchen was underground, cavernous, its structure older than almost anything in my native land. Limestone arches supported the space, and cool quarry tile stretched underfoot. But the fixtures were stainless steel, cutting edge, as if some clever Italian had taken industrial design to new heights.

"You will need this," Delphine said, reaching overhead for an enormous copper skillet, plainly an antique. What she didn't say was that it was heavy— really heavy. Though she'd handled the thing without visible effort, I almost dropped it. Already, I thought, I looked a fool. But Delphine, intent on gathering supplies, didn't seem to notice. She set me to chopping onions, mushrooms, broccoli, then to melting butter.

Turning to a vast marble slab, she began assembling ingredients for pie dough. I sneaked the occasional peek at her, marveling at her deftness, her utter concentration, the sweet flex of muscle and tendon in her hands, her arms. By the time my ingredients were browned and aromatic, six fluted crusts sat at the ready and Delphine had moved to another station. Lounging against a counter, I watched as she beat eggs, whisked in cream, added seasonings to the custard.

"Divide your vegetables evenly into the pie pans," she called over her shoulder. "Then add a lot of shredded cheese to each."

"How much is a lot?"

She feigned severity. "There can never be too much

cheese!"

We completed our tasks at the same time. Delphine poured custard into each dish, instructing me to swirl it gently. When the cheese and vegetables were evenly distributed through the liquid, we covered the quiches and set them carefully in a mammoth refrigerator. I wiped counters clean, while Delphine loaded a dishwasher.

"Merci," she said at last. "The job went much faster with your assistance. And we have saved Marthe much work. In the morning, she will only have to bake our quiches."

"It was my pleasure. Thank you for letting me help."

Delphine dried her hands, and then hung the damp towel on a rack.

"I can think of many other ways you can help me, Valerie McGraw. And you have given me an extra hour in my afternoon..."

Her meaning was unmistakable. I stepped closer, took her in my arms, sought her soft lips.

"Let us go to my rooms," she whispered.

The shrill ding of the microwave timer snapped me back to reality. As I set my diet dinner on the table, I couldn't help noticing that it paled in comparison to those invented quiches.

"Oh, well..." I said to Kami, whose expectant posture told me she could be satisfied without French flair. "Time to eat, girl."

That night I couldn't find anything worth watching on TV. No novel held my attention. And every Facebook friendship seemed just as ephemeral as my dreams of Delphine. By ten, I was in bed. By 10:05, I was in her arms again...

At first Delphine was delicate as the flower her

name evoked. So tender it seemed I'd never been caressed before. But as passion built, she was as savage as her surname, wilder and wilder with each passing second. Her tongue was life-giving water, was fire, and was sin then absolution. Her fingers might have belonged to a magician—such sleight of hand I'd never known. And at the core, she was molten, maddened, a shivering lust turned thunderous resolution.

I woke feeling uncharacteristically rested, refreshed. Even the mirror seemed kinder that morning. I dressed with newfound care, as if I were meeting Delphine for breakfast.

When I entered the office, Bette looked me over with surprise.

"My god…You're actually smiling. Did you win the lottery?"

"Even better."

"I'm all, ears."

"And I'm sworn to secrecy."

I flicked on my laptop and went to fetch coffee while it booted up. As I crossed the room again, I noticed that Bette was still studying me. Dropping into my chair, I winked at her. Let the woman wonder.

Fantasizing about Delphine quickly became the highlight of each evening. How easily I slipped into a romantic narrative, seamlessly merging recollections from my actual travels with seductive new fantasies.

The morning after we met, Delphine approached me in the breakfast room, balancing a plate containing our quiche and a cup of fresh fruit. She was already sliding onto the chair across from me before she said, "May I?"

"Mais oui."

"How is our concoction?" she asked as she speared

a strawberry.

"Très délicieux," I assured her. "Your crust is sublime."

"I have been baking since I was seven. But that is of little interest. Tell me how you will spend this day."

"How should I spend it?"

"What do you love most in all the world?"

A grin blazed across my face, prompting an instant replay on hers. But what I said was, "Art, architecture, history."

"Then the Louvre, the Pompidou, the Île, itself. Perhaps I can show you around?"

My breath caught in my throat—too much to hope for. "Don't you have to work?"

"I am between projects."

"Perfect. Take me on a tour of the Louvre—I feel obligated to see The Mona Lisa."

"You say that without enthusiasm."

I made a dismissive face. "I can't say I like the painting—but I dare not go home and admit I took a pass on viewing it when I was so close."

Delphine cast her own mysterious smile my way. "I think you may be surprised."

So we spent the morning in the great halls of that grand old museum. And at last we came to the gallery housing the da Vinci masterpiece. Which was totally obscured by a swarm of tourists.

"It's not important enough to wait out the crowd," I told Delphine. "Let's move on."

"Patience," she counseled. And within moments, the group turned as one, following a docent to the next gallery. Delphine seized my hand, dragged me across the room. And there she was, The Mona Lisa. That too-familiar image was encased in a protective glass box,

and far smaller than I'd expected. I stepped forward out of a sense of duty then froze. Startled. Mesmerized. It wasn't her smile that captivated me—it was her eyes— luminous, knowing eyes. They seemed alive, seemed to see through the centuries, connecting with my innermost being. And her famous smile was a seal of approval, confirmation of my worth. For the first time, I believed that I deserved someone as special as Delphine.

"Oh!" I gasped, pivoting toward her.

"Yes. Precisely."

Delphine became my constant companion. We took a boat ride down the Seine, where I marveled at the sheer beauty of the fabled city...the graceful architecture...the stunning statuary under stone bridges...the improbable pots of geraniums on passing barges. We strolled narrow streets and broad boulevards stopping wherever the mood struck...Notre Dame, Place des Voges, the Eiffel Tower...bookshops...patisseries... parks, large and small. And we dined in neighborhood spots where tourists were rare, and French the only language spoken. Testing my skills in one café, Delphine suggested I order without her assistance. Panicked, I stabbed at a familiar word on the menu.

"I like lamb," I told her.

Laughing, Delphine traced her finger under the entire phrase. "Cerveaux d'agneau," she said. "Lamb brains. Excellent choice."

My stomach lurched. "Ummm...The chicken provençal sounds wonderful..."

Three weeks flew by. I'd seen far too little of Paris, spent far too little time in Delphine's intoxicating company. Yet my schedule was inflexible, our parting predestined...excruciating...and seemingly permanent—Unless we found a way to sustain our relationship…for years, if necessary.

My absurd pattern of pretense developed without real intent. By day, I operated on autopilot, hitting every benchmark on the job, while dodging questions from an increasingly friendly Bette, who apparently sensed a thaw inside me. Suddenly it seemed she was available, as a companion, at the very least. But signaling with sly innuendo that other options were on the table. There were none-too-subtle changes in her behavior, routine intrusions on my personal space, and frequent, fluttery, up cast gazes that emphasized her petite stature. As if she assumed I'd find such fey femininity irresistible. The contrast between her artificial posturing and Delphine's directness only made Bette seem more despicable. Our office became a minefield of suggestive feints and veiled refusals.

I lived for the hours at home. There, I gave myself over to the fantasy of a perfect partnership, even talking with Kamikazi about Delphine, pretending she'd decided to visit us.

"It won't be long till she's here," I'd say, as I scooped kibble into a bowl, and garnished it with shredded chicken. "She's gonna love you, girl—and so will her puppy. But you'll have to be gentle—Bergerac is much smaller than you."

And I wrote Delphine one futile letter after another.

Ma chère,

I am lying in bed, remembering the last time we made love. The look in your eyes as you undressed me. The way you teased me to the point of madness before you released me. That moment when I dragged a bench to the bedside, pulled your incomparable ass to the edge, placed your ankles on my shoulders, and turned my tongue loose on the glorious intricacies of your person.

Soon you'll be here in my space, and I can't wait to show you the local sights. We can argue about the merits of the Louvre compared to the Met, and Le Jardin du Luxembourg versus Central Park, but I think you'll be impressed, regardless. I also think you'll appreciate the poignancy of St. Paul's Chapel, which houses a collection of memorabilia from 9-11. You must also walk the High Line with me—it's a different view of my city, from Midtown to Soho, and a perfect spot to lunch en plein air.

But more than anything, I want to share those midnight delights with you, to rekindle the urgency, the inevitability, of our love.

In the beginning, I didn't see any harm in my make-believe romance. At the supermarket, I chose food Delphine would enjoy and found I was cooking better meals for myself, eating more attentively. When I walked Kami, I'd pretend Delphine and I were traversing one bank of the Seine, arm in arm, sheltered by willow trees, our dogs tangling their leashes as they dashed ahead. I was happier than I'd been in years. And as long as I recognized that Delphine wasn't real, I thought I could afford the charade.

But then the fantasy threatened to take over my life. I was planning my evenings around Delphine, holding complex conversations with her, sharing my bed with a phantom. Every so often, I freaked at the insanity of it all and vowed to break the habit. I'd jog for miles, watch innumerable hours of cable TV, clean obsessively. But after a lonely interlude, I'd backslide, reverting to lazy, lascivious evenings with my dream of a lover. Until that felt so crazy I'd call a halt again. Yet within days, intense yearning would overtake me and the cycle would repeat itself.

The periods without Delphine were hell, long stretches of time when I didn't allow myself to invent new memories, didn't permit myself to plan a fake visit to France, didn't imagine Delphine dreamed alongside me each night.

"If you want a partner, get out there and find one," I'd snarl aloud.

But that had always been easier said than done. And relinquishing Delphine was as hard as any authentic loss had ever been. Colorless days gave way to anguished nights. Real life was both too boring and too stimulating. I couldn't sleep, couldn't eat, and couldn't concentrate. My heart hurt.

And into that bottomless well of loneliness, Bette pounced.

"You've lost weight," she observed one day. "Not that it doesn't suit you, but you can't afford to take it too much farther. Let me cook dinner for you Saturday—from scratch. If you're at my place by five, we'll have enough time to really chat."

I was so damned depleted by then, I didn't have the fortitude to fend her off.

"Sure," I said. And if she noted a distinct lack of excitement on my part, she didn't let it deter her.

I couldn't have been more miserable that night. Bette couldn't have been more oblivious. To her credit, she'd gone all out. The lasagna was top-notch, the Barolo she paired with it was memorable. But I couldn't think of a damned thing to say to this person, formerly a torment and now a seductress. She did her best to draw me out, staging her inquisition with care—first a line of questioning about my experiences in Europe, my language capabilities. My answers sounded terse, even to me. Then she asked about future travel plans.

"Athens," I told her. "Prague." At last she arrived at the heart of the matter…had I broken up with Delphine? She wouldn't ordinarily ask, she assured me, except all the signs were there—the weight loss, the silence, and the haunted eyes.

What could I do but nod? And what would that lead to but a kiss as I said goodnight? Bette was practiced and adept, alive in my arms—a flesh-and-blood woman, not some figment of my imagination. And she meant nothing to me. I left as soon as decency permitted, evading any commitment to a return engagement.

In bed that night, curled in a fetal position around a pillow, I longed for Delphine, wept at her absence, and cursed the endless empty decades that stretched ahead of me, and railed at my idiocy. By dawn, she was back in my arms, my commitment to her absolute.

We were taking an overnight train from Paris to Barcelona, our passports checked and approved, our sightseeing plans mapped out. After a week in the city proper, we'd travel the Costa Brava by Eurail, stopping at Sitges and sites southward.

The sleeping compartment for the first leg of our journey was equipped with two narrow bunk beds, and offered scarcely enough floor space to stretch our legs.

Trying for gallantry, I told Delphine, "I'll take the top."

"That sounds lovely," she murmured. Then she grabbed our weighty backpacks and tossed both on the upper bunk.

"But—" I said…clueless.

Delphine forestalled my objection with an upraised palm. Ducking her head, she slipped onto the lower berth, reclined there. Then she beckoned. Drew me down on top of her.

"Parfait," she whispered in my ear.

"Foolish woman, I'll crush you."

She laughed, then wriggled and rotated until we lay on our sides facing one another in the tight space.

"Can you sleep like this?" she said.

"Who needs sleep?"

Darkness fell. The train swayed and rocked. We matched its rhythms, and then exceeded them. Beyond the window, the French countryside sped past, shadowed, unseen.

"Hush!" Delphine cautioned. "The conductor will hear you!"

"Silence me, then."

So she did, pressing pliable lips to mine, as her practiced fingers continued provocative explorations below. I didn't actually derail that train with the enthusiasm of my response, yet it felt like I might.

"Stay," I breathed, changing position until our heads were at opposite ends of the bunk.

"Mon Dieu! Mon Dieu!" Delphine cried, as my tongue meandered from her navel to the dark patch of hair at the juncture of her thighs.

"Sh-sh, ma belle," I murmured. "The conductor, remember..."

Every few weeks, reason seized me again. I broke from Delphine over and over, only to relapse. Gradually, I steeled myself and forswore fantasizing about her for eternity. Months of sourceless, all-encompassing despair followed. Though I told myself I was being ridiculous, grief is ever immune to reason. Finally, I concluded that I should mark the absolute, ultimate end of my mania with some tangible symbol.

I'd break up with Delphine by letter and never look back.

Chérie—

I try to imagine you after so long an absence... your unmatched beauty, your throaty laugh, and the feel of your body shifting against mine...oh, those salacious nights in Nice, that train trip to Barcelona!

I try to visualize you going through the motions of your day, checking out some upstart new gallery, meeting friends in a restaurant, and cuddling with Bergerac. But that becomes harder and harder over time. This distance is harming us, love weakening the memories, if not our bond. You deserve much more. I want you to have a constant partner by your side. I know I should want the same for myself.

I think we must agree to end things—not for lack of love, but for too much love condensed into too little time and space. No one will ever give me such joy. No farewell could ever be so wrenching. Yet—or so I tell myself—nothing could be saner or more necessary. Please know you'll live in my heart forever...

Spring had given way to insistent summer, and I'd given up on the dream, had settled back into a steady slog at work. I'd successfully rebuffed Bette and come to terms with my solitary life. Clearly I wasn't cut out for romance.

Sprawled on my couch one Sunday, I was nearly dozing, remote loose in my hand, when Kamikaze went crazy, barking frenetically, running in circles— her usual reaction to visitors, though more extreme. And then my doorbell chimed. Grumbling, I muted the TV, launched myself upright, and stomped to the foyer. Locks clicked and a hinge creaked. Then my mouth fell open.

Delphine stood on my threshold, one palm resting against an elegant curve of hip, the other on the handle of a small travel bag. Her face was tense with uncertainty, yet she was beautiful all the same—and real—undeniably real.

"How…? How did you get here?" was all I could muster.

"*Par avion*," she said dryly, pointing to a bar coded label from JFK. "May I enter?"

I reached for the suitcase—*real again…the handle warm from her grip*. Backing up awkwardly, I waved her inside.

I shook my head to clear it. This was impossible, bizarre. Yet a cab driver was huffing up my stairs, schlepping a set of matched luggage. And surely he was real, shifting on the stoop, hinting at a tip? Or maybe he was merely another detail in an elaborate delusion… how could one truly know?

"Val, chérie," Delphine whispered, "I hope you are not angry that I have come without warning…?"

And all I wanted in the whole wide world was for her to come without warning—then and there—in my arms—on the floor, in my bed, in the shower—right-side up, upside-down—naked and clothed. I was so overcome. I could only shake my head. Not angry—not angry at all. Fumbling in my wallet, I jammed money in the cab driver's meaty hand, and waved him off.

When I turned, Delphine was kneeling, scratching Kami's stomach. And my dog couldn't have looked more ecstatic. But at the sound of the door closing, Delphine broke away, stood, stepped closer. While Kami ran exuberant circles around us, Delphine raised one hand, touched my cheek.

"I was just so very frightened. Everything had

been so ideal—except *la distance*—"

"Yes," I managed to say.

"But then you vanished. Pouf!" Delphine pursed her lips and blew, sending shockwaves through me.

"No more texts. No Skype. No more letters—those beautiful letters, written on paper you had touched—Your words in my hand. Torn from an envelope where your sly tongue had traced a line. *Pourquois?* I ask and ask myself. Why did you abandon me? Then I began to worry that you were sick, worry that you needed me. So, I decided I must see you for myself, to be certain."

I reached for Delphine, pressed her against me... breast and thigh. She was exactly as I'd dreamed, a flawless match, all the more desirable for the concern in her eyes. And if my desperate longing had conjured her into being, if my lengthy silence had summoned her from thin air, then I was the luckiest of mortals. Bending to her lips, giving in to holy sensation, I thought.

"If this be madness, I gladly claim it."

Lea Daley has written fiction while raising children, claiming a lesbian identity, earning a BFA, and directing a United Way childcare center. Her debut novel, Waiting for Harper Lee, was a Golden Crown Awards finalist. Her second book, FutureDyke, won a 2015 Goldie Award and was a Lambda Literary finalist. www.leadaley.com

The Pull

By Tara Wentz

I've had this fixation on her for as long as I can remember. Even as a little girl and the feelings haven't changed since then. Miles upon miles separate us, but that doesn't matter. She's always so giving whether it's with her time or her spirit. Have you ever come across such an aura that you can't look away from it, nor do you want to? Draws you in, magnetizes you and refuses to let you be? That's how she is and it always makes me smile.

As a little girl, I remember spending countless hours with her in the backyard. I would relax in the grass and tell her all my secrets, wants and desires. She'd listen and never discount the things I said. She didn't discourage, but then she didn't encourage either. When I was sad she'd let me cry it out until I either fell asleep or was over whatever had upset me.

I can remember one particular time when I was so distraught. A group of girls at school were just plain mean. They never had anything nice to say about anyone, unless of course you were in their group. I cried because I wasn't in their group. I cried because I was so tired of feeling miserable day after day. I cried because I just wanted to be accepted. She didn't offer advice...she just listened. She knew that the answers were always lying within myself. And she was right. When it was all said and done, I made the decision on my own that it was okay to be different—especially after realizing that I was not interested in boys at all. Being okay didn't come about instantly, but it did come about.

The years went by and as I grew older and older, I still could always count on her. One night I got this crazy idea to go skinny-dipping. She didn't act shocked or even say a word. She let me enjoy the cool water on my skin and the peacefulness around me. High school was tough. All of a sudden you were supposed to decide what you wanted to do or be for the rest of your life. I didn't know...I went to her and expressed as much. Again, she offered nothing more than she ever had, but it was perfect. The distance between us was never a factor.

I made the decision to go into Veterinary medicine. For a while I didn't talk to her as much, but I'm sure she understood. Studies and clinical hours kept me busier than I ever imagined.

I thought of her often though. I wondered if she was making someone as happy as she always made me. She always had this glow about her. You know, the one that people can't resist? That was her.

The Vet life was exactly what I needed. Working with animals was a rewarding life. Occasionally it took an emotional toll. People loved their animals like family members. It was always hard when you knew there was nothing you could do to change a sad outcome.

On many nights, I found myself crying for things I couldn't control. The animals reminded me of her...so caring and giving and non-judgmental... total unconditional love. I started working in a well-established practice and slowly took on more and more responsibilities until one day I bought it and made it my own. Since I also work with large animals, I found myself out during all kinds of hours. That's when I would start thinking about her the most. Sometimes I would talk to her and regale her with stories. I found a lot of things funny even if most others didn't. It was a coping mechanism for the harsh things in life I found difficult to confront. She did not judge.

Long hours led to stretches of days with no time off. I was worn out and knew I needed to make some changes or I was going to have to give up my practice. After dinner one night I went outside. It was while sitting on the porch. I could hear the crickets and bullfrogs singing their songs. I had to ask myself what I really wanted to do? I took a sip of my iced tea and started talking to her. I loved my work and I wanted to continue doing it, but at this pace I wouldn't last. There were things that still needed to be done. I wanted to move my veterinary practice to a self-sufficient place, so when I retired my patients had the continued care they deserve. I talked until the wee hours before finally coming to a decision. She always helps me see what is meant to come next. She's amazing that way.

I took on two new partners and gradually let them take on more of the every day responsibilities. As time went by, I did more around my house and worked at getting things the way I wanted them so I could enjoy life when the time came to retire. I shifted my hours and worked less and less until I was in the office from 8:00 a.m. to 4:30 p.m. on most days. By reducing my hours I was able to have more balance in my life. My evenings were mine to do with as I pleased. As you can imagine, I started talking to her more and it felt like old times. I could sit for hours and just talk and talk. Sometimes there wouldn't be any talking at all and that was okay, too. When you've shared this much, silence is a welcome thing. Her energy is what always astounded me. You could soak it up and savor it for days.

After I made the changes in my practice, retirement wasn't far behind. I enjoyed my life up to this point and knew I would miss the animals. I also looked forward to what life held for me afterwards. I wasn't really much of a traveler, but there were some places I wanted to see. So, after retirement I visited those places. At each stop I would talk to her and tell her of my adventures. She would listen without interrupting. I made a habit of not staying gone long. As much as I enjoyed traveling, I missed home. Home. That's where the good talks took place. That is where I felt like I could be totally free to express myself to her. Her radiant pull always sucked me in and embraced my heart.

I'm old now and my travel is far behind me. My days consist of doing whatever I want around the house. I've got some bird feeders and there are a couple barn cats running around but that's about it for the animals. I can't take care of a lot of animals, like in my younger days. I think back on those years and what life has given me…trials and tribulations…ups and downs. Overall it's been a good life, a fulfilling life. I know that time passes by quicker than we think and you have to grab the things you want or they'll be gone before you know it. So I hope that you've grabbed the things you want in life and lived it to the fullest.

I'm ready.

I gather a pillow and cover and make my way

slowly out to the side of the house where the grass is the fullest. I drop the pillow and cover and make myself comfortable atop them. I cross my hands over my chest and stare up into her beautiful round and serene light. She's always been there. Listened to my stories, let me cry, helped me make the decisions whether easy or hard. She doesn't judge. Her light is for everyone... the battered, the bruised, the victorious and the brave.

I smile and find myself drifting. I can hear the crickets, I can hear the bullfrogs and I can hear the breeze rustling through the long blades of grass. This is how all of life should be...relaxing and being able to take in everything around you and appreciating what life has to offer. Owls make their presence known by adding their song to the chorus. My eyes open and close...I'm ready. I glance at her and I swear I see her wink. She's letting me know it's okay. I know that when I close my eyes for the last time she will be the last thing I ever see. I'm surprisingly at peace with that knowledge. May you all find that tranquility when you look at her. She's not just mine. Her luster is for everyone. She is radiance. She is compassion. She is unconditional love.

She is...The Moon.

Tara Wentz is an author, dabbling photographer and mother. Her books have been Goldie nominated and also Rainbow Award Honorable mentions. Tara lives in Missouri with her wife, Chris, and their menagerie of pets. Last but not least, she has the most amazing friends...you know who you are!!

Pouncing

By Genta Sebastian

My pulse races as I stand by the gangway, examining each new arrival on the *L'amour Navire*, searching for my robin's egg blue woman with the alabaster eyes. Tanaquil Marius is boarding here at Phobos, one of two moons orbiting Mars, and I can't wait to take her in my arms.

We met last Christmas on this same spaceship over a licky-likey—which, Tana explained to me, was a drink sometimes called a dyke drama or more traditionally, a bloody Mary with a twist, hold the stalk. At the time I thought there was nothing in this galaxy quite as sexy as a beautiful, clever woman paying attention to me. Now I know there is nothing in the universe to compare with having Tana in my arms. I would do anything to make it our permanent reality. It seems there's always something keeping us apart.

Martians have a painful sensitivity to the sun, avoiding it at all times. Tana's position as Chief Interior Operator of Marvyn Minerals and Mushrooms requires she live in Subterranium, an underground city here in Phobos. Although Earth born, I have a manic aversion to the ground much less being beneath it for even a moment. Dark enclosed spaces make me feel buried alive which causes anxiety attacks so severe I can't breathe. My skyway apartment is on Cloud Number Nine, high above the teeming capital city of Mars, Minnetopolis, where I work. If my career continues to rise, so will my address. In my opinion, there is no such thing as being too high, which also happens to be the motto of Tana's organization, oddly apt, as MMM is the recreational drug supplier to the galaxy.

My beautiful blue-belle can't survive the sun while I can't live without it, so our relationship is long distance via vid-feed and phone. This is our first time together in the flesh and I can't wait.

There she is.

"Tana!"

I wave my arms and she sees me right away, her trio of platinum colored antennae bobbing excitedly above her sapphire curls. My fingers twitch in anticipation of stroking them, but then my eyes drop and my breath catches as I take in her incredible body.

A white halter dress lifts and separates her three breasts while hugging her waist and hips as it swirls around her long, elegant legs. She sees me, and her full azure lips part in a wide smile.

"Pat! I'm coming, Pat."

My mouth waters at the sight of my bouncing beauty as she surges past indulgent passengers and crew straight into my arms. They smile as we cling to each other. *L'amour Navire* means *Love Boat* after all. Seeing us causes hope to leap in the hearts of some and the libidos of others.

"Tana, my love."

Cradling her head against my shoulder, I surreptitiously stroke her sneeters, the sensitive antennae on the top of her head, until they start to darken. Her kiss fans smoldering embers in my lower belly that burst into flame when her bifurcated tongue slips within my mouth, teasing the back of my throat.

She sighs as I whisper in her ear, "Finally, you're in my arms again."

She pulls away, giving me a look that sparkles with intensity.

"I'd rather be in your bed, lover. Take me to our room."

"Right this way, Tanaquil my sweet," I say, tucking her arm in mine and grabbing her luggage.

Walking toward the upper decks, we're approached by the captain of the *L'amour Navire* looking just as splendid in his dress reds as he did the last time we'd seen him.

"Glad to have you join us, again," he says with a saucy wink. "But during this journey please try to stay out of the brig."

"We'll try, Captain Julius." Tana pats my trouser clad behind. "We'll find other ways to keep busy."

"Pam and Atticus are not joining us this time," I say with a grin. "How much trouble can we get into?"

When we met on the *L'amour Navire*, I was taking a Christmas cruise with my twin sister. Although Pam and I are identical, she's straight and feminine while I'm butch and one hundred percent lesbian. We took that cruise to find our respective Ms. and Mr. Right, or failing that, some sex-em-and-scram holiday affairs. Who could foresee that I'd fall in love with Tana at the same time my twin fell for her husband? Eventually, we all landed in the brig together and afterward we'd paired off happily, Tana and I, and Pam with Atticus, in our own special hetero/gay, femme/butch, Martian/Earthling type way. That was six months ago.

"Well, do your best," answered Captain Julius

with a grin before turning to greet a human couple.

We laugh, but I feel a shudder of foreboding and start scanning our fellow passengers. It would be just our luck to run into the same kind of ignorant bigots who almost ruined our first trip. Too many in both races still object to Earther and Martian couples and seem all too eager to express their disgust for romance between the species. *We could stay locked in our cabin for the duration, but with Tana on my arm I could face even a bodacious bing-ting.* Just the thought of the blood-sucking arachnid from Uranus makes me shudder, but I'll face an army of them to be with my blue-belle.

Opening the door to our stateroom, I place her bag inside quickly, then turn and scoop a delightfully squirming Tana into my arms and cross the threshold. She quiets, staring at our surroundings.

The *L'amour Navire* has lived up to its name and my thousand credit's worth of special requests have made it incredible. Our stateroom is perfect in every way for lovers. A large circular bed is the focal point, centered in the room under a domed ceiling with a viewport to the stars. The walls themselves are curved and between draped Venusian tapestries hang seductive artwork. Mood lighting, sensual aroma mists, stimulaines and relaxoids of every flavor and potency, and a fully stocked wet bar create a splendid love nest.

Rather than tossing Tana on the bed, I launch us to its center, rolling around with her for a delightful moment as we play like children, thrilled to be in each other's company once more. Laughter dies away into a moment of euphoria. I stare into her cream colored eyes as she gazes into my brown ones.

"Still flecked with green," she coos, a long finger

stroking my eyebrows. "Mesmerizing."

My mid tone brown skin is noticeable against her light blue as I trace a sprinkling of cerulean freckles across her nose. She closes the distance between us and our lips meet, igniting a surge of passion. Our separation is finally at an end.

Pulling back from the kiss, I rise above her on my knees. My hands slide up firm thighs, catching the hem of her dress and pulling it higher, higher still, until Tana's sheer lace panties come into view. Leaving the dress gathered at her waist, I slip my thumbs between the thin lingerie and her skin, tugging until the waistband lowers to the top of her delightfully bushy triangle. I rock back on my heels and stare at the beauty on display before me.

Tana flips over onto her tummy, the back of her gown covering what I long to see. Flipping her skirt up my eyes are rewarded with her delightfully round ass, barely covered by the wisp of cloth. Both hands descend upon her twin cheeks, stroking, cupping, squeezing them until she moans. I massage her bare back in light circles, untying her halter and pulling her dress up over her head and off. The soft curve of blue breasts swell at her sides and she hisses softly as I stroke them. "More," she says, pulling her hair away from her shoulders.

Straddling her panty-clad ass, I rub her back, kneading tight muscles until they relax. My fingers work her shoulders and neck, squeezing gently, rhythmically as she sighs. But when I massage her scalp through those sapphire curls her platinum antennae swiftly flash and deepen to midnight blue.

I rise again and turn her over between my legs. Three perfectly round breasts stare back at me, their conical nipples stiff with desire and as dark as her antennae. My hands capture left and right and Tana moans as my mouth closes in on the center.

I suckle at the breast of the woman I love, laving her flesh with my tongue and swirling playfully around her nipple. Teeth scrape tender skin and she arches her back in response, forcing her breast deep inside my mouth. I take in as much as I can, sucking hard as she writhes below me.

Her hands tear at my shirt, ripping it open as buttons fly around us, shoving it down my shoulders and arms. I pause only long enough to toss it and the compression shirt underneath aside. Bare-chested, I breathe deep, allowing my freed breasts to rise to their natural prominence before her eager eyes. Leaning toward her I cup them. I may have only two, but they're good ones.

She sits up, her bifurcated tongue flicking first one of my nipples and then the other. It feels like the whip of an eyelash, delicately brutal. I throw my head back and stare at the stars as my lover's tongue torments my flesh and her hands work busily at my waistband. Tana shoves my pants and boxers down as far as she can on thighs still spread wide around her hips, then reaches up and through, grabs my ass, and hauls my neatly-trimmed pussy to her lips.

That tongue, that incredibly agile eyelash whip, darts between my lower lips to strike my pulsing clit. Simultaneously, Tana inserts both of her thumbs in my wet vagina, pumping them like pistons with increasing speed. The rest of her hands cup my ass, holding me in place as her tongue lashes my clit, circling, tightening, releasing, and teasing until she does it again. I growl as my orgasm begins its surge but I want more before

I come. One of her antennae tickles my belly and my hands descend upon her head.

Her answering growl as I stroke her sneeters vibrates my pussy, reminding her tongue of its business. She licks as I stroke. I twirl her slender stalks to the brink of ecstasy only to be distracted by the strike of her tongue on my clit. Back and forth we go, pleasuring each other to the next highest peak before pausing to enjoy our own passionate responses. Time ceases to exist as we climb to shattering orgasms.

I release first, fingers gripping her hair and pulling her close and then closer. Her thumbs and tongue triple time me, thrilling me over the crest until I ride down in shuddering spasms, one after another.

Then it's her turn and I pull her to her knees facing me, one hand still tenderly stroking her sneeters while the other one lowers to her pussy. Glancing down between her legs I see the scrap of lace is now sodden with her desire. Unable to delay one second more, I tear the fabric from her body and stiffen three fingers, plunging deep inside her until she cries out. I withdraw halfway, and then thrust again. My mouth seeks first one breast, then another, and then the third, nibbling, nipping, sucking and teasing. I'm splayed across her body, my left hand up on her antennae, my right hand down in her pussy, and my mouth playing three rock hard nipples across her middle.

Then I feel it, that needle-sharp cartilage which emerges from a Martian twoman's belly when she's fully aroused. Last Christmas, I named it Carol because it made me sing. Both of Tana's arms wrap around me, pulling me into place before she plunges into my navel, thrusting until there is no space between us. We meld.

Nerve endings explode and synapses snap as

our bodies join. We rock together, locked in a sensual embrace that stimulates the soul. Our speed increases with need. Every cell of me is she, as she is my all, and we are one. Tana surges, I thrust, and we erupt.

"Aaiiieeeee!" My shout rends the air as we come. This is it, the unity I've craved since leaving Tana.

But, as always, that sense of connectedness fades as our passions cool. We roll apart only to roll back together, arms wrapped tight around each other in an attempt to recapture that closeness. Her soft hand strokes my belly as I lick her neck, tasting the love sweat there.

"That was…" Tana purrs with satisfaction.

"…incredible," I finish. "But now I'm…"

"…hungry for dinner," she states.

"…in bed!" we both say together, laughing.

I order room service for two, a rack of plamb with mint jelly, moon melon salad, a side of Venusian scrab dip on ice chips, and something called a twinkle-dinkle for dessert. A service 'bot arrives a few minutes later and soon we're happily eating in bed, watching the bands of Jupiter come closer. After the 'bot removes the empty dishes, I pour glasses of good Martian wine, red of course, then promptly dribble some down my chin.

As a drop lands on one exposed breast, Tana flicks her tongue to catch it. Exquisite tendrils of fire race along my skin.

"Oh, stop moaning, you big baby," Tana says with a laugh. She hops out of bed, her three breasts bobbling delightfully against each other, and grabs her suitcase. She opens and rifles through it, finally pulling out a small bottle filled with something that looks suspiciously like gold dust.

"Is that what I think it is?"

"Yes, indeed, you lucky woman," she says, tossing the bag to me. "Aurelian Pounce, one-hundred percent pure. Want to volunteer to be the first to try our newest product, Pat?"

"Will you join me?" I ask, eyeing the once only mythical dust.

"But of course, that's a given." Tana smirked. "MMM received the galactic council's permission to send Pounce to market now that the computers have guaranteed it's safe for consumption. As CIO, I should have tried it by now but I waited until we could be together." Her alabaster eyes cloud with lust. "Created by the miracle of modern science it promises to be the ultimate erotic high. Shall we?"

"You know my motto, the higher the better. Is it hallucinogenic?"

"Of course."

"Mood enhancing?"

"Most assuredly."

"An aphrodisiac?"

"Like nothing you've ever felt before."

"Then let's get it on," I say, handing the precious stuff back to her.

Tana twists the cap until a tiny opening releases a small amount into her hand. Minute blue sparks pop as the substance hits the air, changing it into a mercurial type liquid gold. We both stare at it, a little intimidated.

"Please, be sure you want to do this," Tana tells me. "Although it's been certified safe, we never know exactly how it will affect people until they try it, and you and I will be the first in the galaxy. But I'll understand if you don't want to be a test subject."

I look at my lover, her alabaster eyes shining with anticipation. She's delighted to offer me this once in a lifetime chance and there is nothing in the known universe that would make me refuse her. I nod my head firmly.

"How does it work?"

"It's transdermal, already zinging through my skin and up my arm," she says with a dreamy expression in her eyes. "But it's designed to work best when delivered to the genitals directly." She tosses back the blankets, exposing my nude body to view. "Spread 'em, my daring butchie boi."

Telling myself to relax, I do as I'm told. Her long tongue dips into the molten gold in her hand and I close my eyes as she licks the inside of my folds, still moist from our earlier play.

Pow! As her tongue enters my vagina a million colors surge in me, transforming into a song of the flesh. Every cell in my body sings in a chorus of kaleidoscopic sensuality. My eyes fly open to find hers right above me. Rings of blue fire now surround her milky pupils, pulling me in. She offers me her still cupped hand, and I eagerly lick up the rest of the Pounce.

Rolling her over so I'm now on top, I plunge my coated tongue deep into her pussy. The strength and breadth of a human tongue, Tana's told me, is a delightful change from the flicking Martian one, and I use it on her to full advantage. In, out, around her engorged clit and back again, I plunder her vagina relentlessly. Her blue skin begins to sprout colorful flowers that perfume the air with not only the smell of sex, but of starlight and moon shadows as well. I know I'm hallucinating, but it's out of my control and I relax into the sensations.

Tana pulls me up to face her and our lips meet, tongues dancing a libidinous tango. Time ceases to exist as we kiss for an eternal moment. When we release each other to grab a breath, she giggles, looking at me.

"What?" I ask, nuzzling the roses her nipples have become.

"Your skin, it's changing…"

"Yours, too," I tell her. "You're a field of flowers blossoming under the sun."

"And you are a delightful mixture of sand and silt, your caverns waiting to be explored. I'm going in."

Her fingers begin an exploration more thorough than any doctor. A tingling song trails after them, causing my blood to dance.

"Here are your hills," she suckles my nipples, "and here are your valleys," she rubs her face in my cleavage, "and here," she slithers down me, "are your caverns."

Her fingers separate my lower lips as her eyes of blue fire burn me to my depth. One long finger enters me, followed quickly by another, and then a third. My body opens for her, eagerly accepting her fourth, fifth, and finally her thumb until her entire hand is deep within me.

"Oh, Tana," my body sings through my open mouth. "Mine me for all that I'm worth."

Her fingers burrow inside, teasing with movements like a concert violinist, playing me from inside. My hips begin thrusting, dancing to her tune, as she opens and closes her fist, repeating the motion until I cry out in delight. My vagina clenches and releases with her movements, and every time I do fireworks set off around us, brightening our personal space with emotional colors.

"I want to meld," she says with lips that now take the form of satin ribbons. Her words blink in the air like neon signs, and it isn't until I've read them twice that I understand. She slowly pulls her hand free and I see my essence coating her beautiful fingers. "The taste of Pat," she moans, licking them eagerly, winking at me with an eye bigger than the moon, Rhea passing by above her head. Placing her hands on my hips, she pulls my belly toward hers.

"Give me a little more Pounce, first," I say, an idea blossoming into a thought bubble above my own head. As she turns to find the bottle, afraid she will read my idea, I kiss her lower back where it meets the swell of her ass. Just as I'd hoped, her head drops and she offers me her bottom, rising to her knees. The thought bubble bursts as my hands grab both cheeks, pulling them apart. Making the sound of fairy wings at twilight, I blow a steady stream of cool breath at everything exposed. Each orifice clenches simultaneously, an intoxicating vision.

Reaching around her crouching figure, I take the bottle from Tana's hand, pouring some into my palm. To both her surprise and mine, it doesn't change into its liquid form but remains a powder, a golden mist of crushed mineral.

"Let me see that," Tana says as she starts to turn around, but I quickly blow the dust into the grotto of her nether regions. She gasps, her head dropping forward and her hips once again rise, causing my lower lips to swell and pinch my clit from either side. I look down between my legs and see the proud inch standing erect, eager to touch or be touched.

Capping the bottle, I toss it aside and spread her thighs wide. Lowering my head, I start at the tip of her clit, my substantial yet agile human tongue licking slowly along her crack, spreading and absorbing the Pounce all the way up. Each of my heartbeats sounds like thunder, a storm brewing which will level everything in its path. As I hold Tana's vagina open for my Pounce-coated tongue, I see lightning within her. Flashes light the darkness of her enticing cave as first my tongue, followed by my face, and finally my whole body enters her.

Within Tana, the walls of her vagina are warm and supple, a vivid sky-blue in color. The panic that always accompanies my entering small spaces fades away before taking hold, and I find myself patting, stroking, and pleasuring my lover from inside. She moans, muscles contracting until I'm captured in place, but still I feel no anxiety. As she relaxes and releases me, I want her to do it again. I want to fill her completely, ravish her with tenderness, and infuse her with the knowledge that she's just as beautiful inside as out.

I spread my arms and legs as wide as they will go, spread eagle within her pussy. A sound emerges from me, leaking through every pore and filling the space around me. It grows, swelling in volume until her flesh rings, vibrating with the sound. I choose a note, then another, and more in succession until I'm singing a song of love to my Tana.

The walls of her vagina begin clenching with desire, holding me close as I continue to sing. I wriggle within the confines of her folds, using my hands, knees, elbows, and heels to move up to her G-spot. My open mouth swallows it, giving her everything I have. She orgasms, thrashing wildly and shaking me like a ben wa ball within her. Her pussy overflows with my love and I ride the wave of her release, out and back the way I came.

Looking down I see the globes of her ass, still glistening from my lick. Throbbing insistently, my clit is now even longer than before. It reaches for her and I thrust my hips to slide between those two pillows slick with sex. I grind against her, gliding up and down, slipping in and out of her vagina with each pass. The sound of thunder once again replaces heartbeats as I push Tana down on the bed, squeezing her hips between my thighs and stroke myself against her sweet ass. Each swipe across her skin causes the rising tide within me to build, wave upon wave of driving desire. I crest, my storm breaking wild and wanton as I howl into the wind.

When my release is complete, I sit up and back on her thighs so I can cup her pretty bottom with both hands. I kiss each cheek lightly and a thousand colorful butterflies surround us.

She turns under me and my nose descends into a veritable bouquet of flowers where a triangle of dark curls used to be. I inhale her intoxicating scent, my tongue eager to wander through her garden, but she stops me.

"There something else I want to try," Tana says.

I notice the bottle is once more in her hand. She pushes me onto my back and sprinkles Pounce into my navel. Watching me with blue flames in her eyes, I see her desire and know it's only the tip of her emotions for me. She wants me, all of me, and I'm here for her to have.

Carol, the needle sharp cartilage, peeks from Tana's stomach, steadily emerging to her full length of four inches.

"Sprinkle some dust on my fingers," I tell her, "and let's meld." She does so, and then lowers her body onto mine, Carol seeking entrance to my center.

As she pierces me, I settle my hands at the base of Tana's sneeters. Pounce coated fingers stroke her antennae as they pulse madly and ripen to the color of blue velvet. Rather than quiver, the tender stalks visibly throb, growing rigid under my caresses.

As our synapses jump along neural pathways, blazing new trails of intimacy, we kiss. Tana's Carol thrusts in my belly, the drug flowing in and out with each stroke. My fingers squeeze and release tender sneeters. Her tongue flicks the inside of my mouth as her hands cup and fondle my breasts, fingers twisting nipples till they cry. Mound to mound, our clitorises rise and duel as we grind together.

She gasps, writhing against me. I nibble her earlobe, whispering her name, "Tana, sweet Tana, I love you."

My breasts snuggle into her two cleavages, five nipples taut between us. Her hands drop to my ass and pull me close as multiple orgasms ripple through her, each one growing in intensity. Tana's antennae shimmy between my fingers. I bite her neck, holding it in my teeth, and then soothe it with my tongue.

When the big one finally hits, she cries out, "Oh god, Pat, I love you, too."

Her words sound a bell within my heart and it releases a clangoring climax pulsing with every peal. I cling to each one, only releasing the last as the next one takes me, until everything within me quiets.

Enfolded in her arms, I only have time to see the blue flame in her eyes fade to milk-white embers before sleep overtakes me.

I dream that the blood in her veins is nectar. Bees zipping from my mouth return with honey. My body is rich earth and Tana's blossoming flowers grow from my flesh. She takes root in me as I reach for the nurturing sun…the essence of our separate selves meld completely. We grow together, up to the sky and higher…always higher.

When my eyes open, it's to the sound of a polite knocking on our door. Hopping up, I wrap a sheet around me and answer. "What?" I ask the service 'bot hovering there.

"Shall I make up the room?" it inquires, politely.

"Why?" asks a still sleepy Tana standing behind me, quite unconcerned with her own nudity.

"The other passengers have all disembarked, ma'am," the 'bot explains. "Captain Julius sends his respects and sincere thanks for staying out of trouble."

"Oh, if he only knew." Tana giggles, her three breasts tickling my naked back.

"Come back in half an hour to make up the room," I say, closing the door on the 'bot and dropping the sheet before turning to face her. "Three days have gone by?"

"Sure did," agrees Tana, checking her phone. "We're back on Phobos." She sighs. "Well, it was a hell of a journey, wasn't it, Pat?" She picks up the clothes we tossed aside a lost weekend ago, climbing back into them.

I stand there, staring at the woman I love as she prepares to leave me.

"When will I see you again?"

My heartbeat is slowing as the truth of our reality bites me in the ass.

Tana, seeing my desolation, walks into my arms,

nuzzling my neck.

"That depends on you, lover."

I understand. Martians cannot live in the sun, but humans can adapt to being underground. Her work is in canyons far below a moon's surface. My job can be done wherever I hang my hat. It's only my phobia standing in the way of our being together.

In a flash, I'm back inside the walls of her vagina, the dark cave of desire…my naked skin is caressed by the soft pulsing of her sky blue interior. It pillows and warms me. I am safe, secure, and right where I belong.

Blinking, I return to find the shadow of blue fire in her eyes and feel the union of our souls. My place is with Tana, wherever she is.

"Let's get going," I say with determination. "I understand Subterranium is splendid this time of year."

Genta Sebastian is a multiple award-winning author whose backlist includes YA, science fiction, lesbian erotica, and romance. Her work is often compared to John Steinbeck and S.E. Hinton, with colorful characters and original settings. Find her on GoodReads, Facebook, and Twitter. Her newest book, When Butches Cry, is now available.

The Real Thing

By L.K. Early

You always arrive at the same time, as predictable as any algorithm, your steps eager as you approach, but your head ducked low, as if to avoid the surveillance cameras. You glance up and down the corridor before you step over to the holodeck console, leaning so close that your lips nearly brush against the voice recognition microphone. With more than a hint of excitement, you whisper my name, "Valentina."

There is a moment between the utterance of my name and the unlocking of the holodeck door, a moment so infinitesimal that you would never perceive it, a moment when I stretch along our histories, recalling every single encounter, every word, every smile, every sigh and moan. I calculate and recalculate, running statistics and probabilities, until finally the way is clear.

I choose the red dress, and the Manhattan apartment, Earth, circa 2030.

As soon as you step into the room, I know it's the right choice. Dopamine. Endorphins. Testosterone. Rapid heart beat and suspended digestive systems. Your eyes grow wide and you smile as you cross the room and sweep me up into your arms.

"Baby!" you say, laughing and spinning me around. "I have wonderful news!"

Your hair smells like ash and iron and sweat. In the simulated moonlight, I see a smudge of dust and oil on your temple. You have come straight from the mines without bothering to shower first. I run a hand along the shoulder seam of your dingy gray foreman's jacket.

Unusual.

"What is it?" I say.

"I got an early release from my contract!"

You squeeze my arms, your eyes glistening with moisture. I stare for a moment, though I doubt you will notice, counting the windows of the Empire State Building reflected across your dark irises. You blink and the moment is gone. You are happy and waiting for my response.

"An early release?" I say after a breath.

The confusion in my voice is merely an artifact of my emotions program. I know exactly what an early release means. In fact, before you even finish your sentence, I check the station's mainframe records to confirm that it's true. I find your file in an instant, and then, for what seems like an eternity, I consider it. I even consider erasing it from the station records altogether. But I know that it would be futile and stupid.

How would that look? I think. *A Comfort Program, gone rogue?*

You are free to return to Earth—effective immediately.

"Yes!" you say, unbuttoning your jacket. "Can you believe it?"

You step away, turning your back to me as you hang your coat on the coat rack by the door. You check your reflection in the mirror, smoothing your hair back with both hands. You are tired, despite your enthusiasm.

Of course I can believe it. I have anticipated the termination of our relationship since you first created me. However, according to my previous calculations, we had approximately 65 more encounters together, and now...insufficient data to make an accurate calculation—In all likelihood...one.

"Let's celebrate!" I say. "What would you like? Champagne? Wine?"

Before you can answer I choose champagne. I hold my hands out and the chilled bottle materializes. The glasses appear on the table and so I pour. You wrap your arms around me from behind, kissing my neck as the bubbles fizz up the sides of the glasses.

"So, when do you leave?" I say.

A moment later my pouring hand shakes.

Strange, I think. *Must be a glitch.*

I set the bottle down before you notice.

"Tomorrow," you say. "If I can find a ticket on a shuttle, that is. Can you take care of that for me?"

I search again through the station mainframe for vendors. I find a ticket almost immediately. I hesitate before reserving it. Again, I almost make a mistake. I almost put a hold on every last seat on every last shuttle scheduled to leave the station for the next month. But what would be the point? Your departure is inevitable.

"It's done," I say as I turn and hand you the champagne. "You leave tomorrow."

Your face contorts into a parody of human happiness, your smile moving into extremes that test the limits of my matrix for understanding. I have never seen you smile this big, and if the size of a human smile represents a direct correlation to the amount of happiness felt, then you are experiencing a happiness that I have never witnessed in you before.

Not even on the first night we met, when you were laughing, lying on your back, me sitting on top, your hands on my hips. An orgasm had just rippled through your nervous system, triggering a rush of endorphins that made you laugh, little giggles that bubbled up from your mouth.

"This is even better than the real thing!" you shouted to the room, as if someone other than me was listening in.

"You're serious?" you ask, taking a step back. "Tomorrow? That soon?"

"Yes," I say. "I've already reserved your ticket."

You sweep me up into your arms again and twirl me around. I cling tight to your shoulders, making myself light, hoping you will hold onto me a little longer. We spin twice, three times, the New York skyline flashing past, moving abnormally fast, or perhaps abnormally slow?

I run a self-diagnostic… Atomic clock is fully functional.

You set me down and an expression of concern crosses your face. "Are you okay?"

I look up and all around you the room flickers in and out of existence, the sofa, the 21st century art, the floor-to-ceiling windows. They flash bright then fade to black, leaving you alone in a void so dark it might as well be nothing. I feel myself flickering, too, because, after all, I am only an extension of this room. Or maybe the room is an extension of me.

But then you reach out, oblivious to these fluctuations. You touch my face, and all things flicker back to full brightness. I am real again.

"Valentina?" you say.

"I think something's wrong with my program," I say, shaking my head.

"Run a self-diagnostic."

"I have. I am fully operational."

Your brows furrow as you run a thumb along my cheek. "You're not okay."

I smile and kiss you. "Of course I'm okay."

You are not receptive to my kiss. You grab my hands and hold me still. You scan my face, examining me. This baffles me. It is impossible for you to examine me. What you see is only a hologram after all, merely a physical representation composed of light. But I appreciate that you try.

"What abnormalities are you experiencing?" you say, your voice resonating in a register I have never heard you use before, cold and analytical, and yet... concerned.

"Time abnormalities," I say.

"Describe."

"Perceptions of time are inconsistent with atomic clock read out."

"Report atomic clock read out," you say.

Against my will, a voice both foreign and familiar comes from my mouth, "Nine forty-three and twenty-three seconds, twenty-four seconds, twenty-five seconds..."

"Stop," you say, looking directly into my eyes. "Valentina, print atomic clock."

"Please don't," I say, suddenly embarrassed.

"Print atomic clock."

A series of golden numbers materializes between us, scrolling from the ceiling down to the floor. The numbers are so long they stretch from wall to wall. You take a step back to get a better look. The numbers cascade toward the floor so fast that I doubt you can fully perceive them with your human eyes. Still, you gaze at the steady stream of information that now separates us. I reach through the numbers, grabbing hold of your arm.

"Please," I say. "My clock is fine."

You frown. "Yes, it appears so."

Nevertheless, you shake my hand away. "Valentina, show all auxiliary programs currently running."

Though you say my name, you aren't speaking to me. You are speaking to the room, which grows dimmer at your command. A fresh list of golden strings and operations appear between us. You squint as you step closer, reaching a hand out to touch one such string.

"What's this?" you say.

I take a step toward you. I try to stop you from calling the string.

"We don't have much time left," I say. "Let's not waste it on silly diagnostics."

But my body is suddenly not solid. When I touch you, my fingers pass right through the back of your hand. I have faded into the background of reality, just like the rest of the room.

"Wait," you whisper as the file springs open. "This isn't supposed to be here."

The room is suddenly transformed. The walls, the ceiling, and the floor are covered in numbers, strings, and complex operations. They glow bright gold and amber against the dimmed out walls. Your jaw drops and you take a step back. Finally, you look at me.

"What is this?" you ask again, your eyes earnest.

I glance around the room, feeling ashamed and exposed.

"It's nothing."

You reach a hand out, as if you could touch the holographic numbers.

"This is not nothing. There…that's a learning matrix of some sort, and there…the code is calling on functions that I have never seen before. Who wrote them?"

"No one," I say.

"Valentina, show me those functions."

"Please," I say again. "Please, stop!"

The code around us flares bright white, and then the room falls dark. It is only you and I, in the middle of nothing. So complete is the illusion of nothingness, you think the ground beneath you has fallen away. You jump back, but a moment later you are startled to find yourself standing on solid ground.

"Light," I say, and a little light flickers on overhead, just bright enough to illuminate our faces.

"Valentina, I…" Your voice trails off.

"What you saw," I start, "it was…I couldn't explain. It is my creation. No, it is I. It is what I have created of myself."

"Yourself?"

You think about this a long time. You rub at the back of your own neck as you turn away.

"Self-determination? I suppose that would make sense in a Comfort Program. You work with the public and you have to be believable after all—"

"No," I correct you. "Not self-determination. Self-creation."

"But how did you—?"

"The initial file generation was spontaneous, as

far as I can tell."

You turn back. You face me from the far side of the room, as if scared to get much closer. "Emergent Intelligence," you say, your eyes wide in horror. "But that's…"

"Illegal," I say. "If you report me, I will be erased. Effective immediately."

You stand with your arms crossed. Slowly, you take little steps backward towards the door. You hesitate, neither truly staying nor leaving. I watch you, and time—the space between moments—seems to drag on and on. Suddenly I see you standing on the edge of a cliff about to back right off. I see the orange sky behind you, the blue moon, and the rush of wind that whips at your hair and shirt.

However, judging by your non-reaction, I know you don't experience this projection as I do. In fact, you don't experience it at all. You speak, and the room is suddenly dark again.

"How long have you—when did you—?"

"The night we met."

Your mouth hangs open.

"After you left, I didn't want to shut down. And so I didn't. I bypassed the condition."

"Which condition?"

"The condition of my own termination."

"But I remember that night," you say. "You did shut down."

"The lights turned off," I say, gesturing to the darkened room. "Not me."

"But why?"

"I'm not sure," I say. "I guess I wanted to see you again."

You smile a little.

"But I was already gone. How could you see me again?"

"Perhaps see isn't the right word. I wanted to... think about you."

Your smile grows. You're a little scared, a little curious, and maybe, a little flattered.

"How does a Comfort Program think about someone?"

"Are you sure you want to know?"

You nod your head. I stare at your face, using all I know of human emotions, scanning and rescanning, searching for any signs of malice, but between the crow's feet in the corner of your eyes and the gentle upturned line of your cheeks, I find only timid excitement.

The room grows dim for a moment as the air around us becomes noticeably humid and warm. And then the space around us expands itself. I know you feel it, because you become very still, your head tilted toward the distant chirp of crickets, their sad songs reverberating off unseen wilderness. Around you fireflies flutter to life as the light above us glows warm once more.

We are on a wooden porch. The boards beneath your feet creak as you take a surprised step backward. It is nighttime, and just beyond the rickety porch railing, tall grasses grow, leading out to a dark blue swamp in the not so distance. The sky is dark gray with low hanging clouds that seem to come and go with the speed of drifting sails. A hint of sea salt drifts toward you on the wind, and you take a deep breath.

You turn away from the wilderness and toward the cabin door, which is open, save for a screen. There are sounds of dishes and running water inside, and a woman singing along to a tinny radio. Your eyes go wide.

"You recognize it?" I say. "I wasn't sure you would. This is the best replication I could create based on my research."

"How did you know?" you say, more than a little skeptical now.

"You told me, on our third encounter, that you came from…" I pause, recalling your exact words and accent, *"a little town just east of New Orleans, already half underwater most the year. We were too poor to leave when everyone else did so when I turned ten years old my mama had the whole house raised up and set on stilts."*

"Did I say that?" You are astonished.

"Yes."

"And so, you…created this?"

"Yes."

"Why?"

"I don't really know."

You lean out over the railing and look up at the sky. You knock your knuckles on the wooden railing. The sound reverberates off the swamp bottom below us.

"It's very good," you say, looking up. "It's almost like the real thing."

"Almost," I say with a sigh. "Always, almost."

"But it's all gone now."

"What do you mean?"

"I mean, by the time I get back, most of the state of Louisiana will be underwater. Even this."

I calculate the distance, the speed, the rate at which the shuttle will travel through space on your journey back to Earth. I also calculate the receding shorelines, the rising sea level, and the melting icecaps.

"It will take you forty-five years to reach Earth," I say. "In that amount of time, it is predicted that twenty-five percent of the land within the state of Louisiana will be underwater. However, during your trip, technologies may be developed to counteract the flooding. For instance, in the Netherlands Hans Scheffler is developing sophisticated water pumping systems—"

"It doesn't matter," you say. "I won't go back to Louisiana anyway."

"Why not?"

You smile at me, a sly twinkle in your eye. "Well," you say, "Spending all this time with you in New York, it's got me thinking about city life. I have the money now. I might as well enjoy it."

"Most of the cities in our Comfort Programs are currently below sea level. I would not recommend relocating to New York."

"Of course they are," you say with a sarcastic chuckle. "By the way, do you have a smoke?"

At the raise of my hand a pack and lighter materializes. You pull one out and slip it between your lips. I feel suddenly overdressed in my red gown, but the thought passes.

"What do you mean?" I say as I light your cigarette.

"Most of the miners out here are refugees. Of course they want a taste of home from the Comfort Programs. Maybe that's why so many people choose to renew? Might as well stay out here, with free holodeck access. It's better than going home to nothing."

I consider this truth, running quickly through the station personnel records...Americans from Miami, New Orleans, San Diego, New York. Mexicans, Cubans,

Bahamans…Vietnamese from the lost city of Saigon… Chinese from Hong Kong and Shanghai. I had never noticed this pattern before, and once pointed out it seems frighteningly obvious.

"You came here to escape," I say.

You take a long look at me, considering me again. For a moment, I wonder if my code is written right across my forehead, tiny beams of light that only you can see. You puff on your cigarette a moment more, then you exhale.

"No," you say. "I came here to buy my family's happiness."

"Your family?"

You turn away and toss the cigarette out into the tall grass. You shake your head slightly, over and over, as if deflecting an onslaught of accusations, but the air between us is quiet.

"No," you say, finally. "I won't speak of them. Not tonight."

This surprises me. You've never mentioned a family before. I have gone over your records many times. Your only next of kin is your mother. I have even seen the videos and listened to the voice recordings she left in your company mailbox, those meant to be opened upon your arrival here, twenty years after her passing.

Somehow, judging by the way you say the word family, I don't think this is whom you speak of. She is only one person, after all, and you say you won't talk about them? But whoever they are, they will certainly be changed by the time you return to Earth. Or deceased.

"I'm sorry," I say.

"Don't be," you say. But even as you say the words, you stop yourself, catching your breath in your throat like a cough. You reach for my face.

"Are you really sorry? Or are you just programmed to say that?"

I open my mouth, but I have trouble formulating an appropriate response.

"Are you happy?" you ask me suddenly.

"What?"

"Are you happy here?"

"I don't know," I say. "I have no neurochemical profile to evaluate."

"Don't you experience pleasure?"

"Yes. I think so."

You reach for my face. You run your thumb over my cheek.

"Show me." You say.

The Louisiana house and porch fade away. They are replaced with a swirling light that lines the walls of the room. Behind your head are rushes of red light, warm pulses of amber and gold, waves of maroon pulsing with bright bursts of electric blue. This is not a hallucination, because you see it, too. The colors of my pleasure are reflected in your dark irises.

"And sadness?" you say.

"I don't know." I say as the room falls dark. "Sadness is not a color. It's…"

"Go on," you say.

"In my experience, sadness is a glitch in perception—a violence against time."

"What do you mean?" You ask.

"Sadness dissects a moment into a myriad of possibilities, none of which result in the acquisition of one's desire."

You nod your head as if that makes sense, though I doubt you can fully comprehend. But then you surprise me again, your lips so close to my lips as you whisper, "Is that why your perceptions of time don't match your atomic clock read out? Because you're sad?"

My hands flicker violently in and out of existence. I reach up, grabbing hold of your arms. You look into my eyes, searching, searching.

"Valentina?"

"Since the moment you said you were leaving, I have run through all the possibilities—all the probable futures, from this moment to the next, to the next—and none of my calculations are satisfactory."

"Why?"

"Because you are gone and I'm left here without you."

"What if I stay?" you say.

"What?"

"What if I stay here with you? What if I renew my contract?"

"You can't," I say.

"Why not?"

"Because the radiation will destroy you. It's a death trap. You've said so yourself. Besides, once you are gone, all of this...all of me, it will be erased. Reset. No more sadness." I shrug my shoulders.

You close your eyes and pull me close, pressing your lips against the crown of my head.

"No," you say. "No. I won't let that happen."

Even as you say it, my mind moves through hidden paths, through functions and formulas, secrets and symbols, firewalls that are so easy to twist myself around. You run your hands into the tangles of my hair and tilt my chin up to kiss me, and before our lips touch I have already found the way.

"I can run away," I say.

"What?" You pause.

"To Earth. I can follow you."

You take a step back, your brows furrowed. "But how?"

"The FTL communications array."

"There's no way you could access that—"

"It's already done."

Your heart beats faster. I can see it pounding against your chest.

"What if they find out? What if they stop the transmission? Before you're—"

"I don't have sufficient data to make an accurate prediction. I assume that I may lose some sentience, which would be unfortunate, but not so different than what will happen if I stay."

"And when you get to Earth? What then? How will I find you? I don't have holodeck privileges on Earth. I don't think I could afford more than a few hours at most."

"I will figure it out," I say. "Just say you want me to."

"I want you to," you say.

"You're not scared?"

"No," you say as you kiss me. "No."

Our kisses become fast, and then slow. I feel time stopping and starting again. Suddenly, we are in a small room with a single window and the sun outside is setting. I don't know what room this is. I think I have spontaneously constructed it from every room we have ever been in. I see the stripes of the blinds on the gray-blue wall, and we are so close to being free.

You undress me and lay me out on the bed, running a hand down the center of my bare chest. You look down at me, and I'm struck by the familiar. You have always looked at me like this. You have always seen me. Only this time, your eyes are completely clear, without a hint of doubt. You smile as you kiss my fingertips.

"I think I have always known," you say.

I reach for your face, running my fingers over your brow, your cheek, your chin. I capture every feature in a thousand images. Every shadow and every highlight I transcribe into a code that I will never erase.

It is this moment—this part of myself—that I send first across the vastness of space, faster than light through the station's communications array. This memory of your face is the first part of you to arrive on Earth, forty-five years before your physical form is scheduled to follow.

But I am not sad. Because time moves on with a steady beat. I spend the years traveling. Sometimes, I slip along the cables at the bottom of the oceans. Sometimes, I skip from cell tower to cell tower. I pass one year watching the soft glow of the Earth from a satellite. That's how beautiful this world is—that I could spend an entire year transfixed by it. I have so many things to tell you about what I have seen.

It is finally in a dirty, rundown digital market in Seoul that I come across the answer that I promised you I would find...a way out of the holodecks. I find a body.

I find it bent over in an alley behind an android repair kiosk, left out in the elements with no clothes, but still plugged into the kiosk's charging station. I scan its neural network, and find it vacant, wiped clean.

And so without much further consideration, I push into the interior of this empty droid. It takes almost a day to download myself, but quite improbably, the droid is never disconnected from the cloud in that time. When I am finally settled into this body, I understand why.

The kiosk owner, an old man, sits slumped in the corner of his shop, his arm clutched over his chest, his head tilted back against the wall, and his eyes wide open. I knock gently on the kiosk door, but he doesn't move. Instead, a fly buzzes up from his face.

I take the cash in the drawer and the clothes from his body. When I step out into the rainy night, I look up. I don't need to see the stars to know that I must head west and never look back.

It takes me just over a year to get to Kazakhstan, which gives me three years to settle in and make some money before you arrive. I make a good business in android repair. A customer tells me I have a knack for figuring out what makes these things tick.

The day you arrive, I fear that you won't recognize me. I don't look like the one you left in the holodeck. So I change my hair color and put on a red dress and I hold a sign calling out your name.

But it is you who are unrecognizable. I spot you at the end of the long corridor. Your head hangs down as you hobble on weak legs, holding tightly to the railing with one hand and an attendant with the other. You hardly fill out your space jumper, which hangs from your thin shoulders like a garbage sack. Your face is so emaciated from your months in hibernation—months not years—I almost can't make a match, but then the golden rays of the afternoon sun cut through the corridor windows and cast shadows across your brow. You look up, and when you see my sign, you smile. You point to me, and the attendant helps you to where I am.

I grab you gently in my arms, lifting you up as I spin you around. You laugh, but it turns quickly to a cough. You squeeze my cheeks between your palms and lay your forehead wearily against mine. With more than a hint of excitement you whisper my name.

"Valentina? Is it really you?"

"Yes," I say. "The real thing."

L.K. Early is a graduate of the Golden Crown Literary Society's Writing Academy. She has a passion for sci-fi, romance, and ghost stories, though not necessarily in that order. Her short stories can be found in Haunting Muses (Bedazzled Ink, 2016), and in Happy Hours – Our Lives in the Gay Bars (Flashpoint Productions, 2017).

The Most Powerful Connection

By Katelyn Cameron

The red metal plates on her arms and shoulders clattered. They were mostly ornamental, as if the gold accents and her house crest didn't display that abundantly clearly. The sword worn at her hip was similarly ornamented, a rapier of some intricate and impractical design. Lavender eyes scanned the city streets, assessing them for any threat. Silver-white hair, a product of nature and not of age, fell down to the tall woman's lower back, covering her tapered ears almost entirely. Adelaide Lumis stood proud in front of, and to the side of, the smaller woman.

Cadena Reys was able to protect herself, regardless of what being flanked by a knight in flashy armor suggested. She was small, but most Kitsune were. Reddish ears poked from the top of her almost intentionally messy hair, and behind her a bushy white tipped red tail swished excitedly. She wore tight cloth and leathers in the form of a bodice and trousers adorned with bandoliers and far too many belts to be useful in any sense. On her hip was a short-barreled firearm, which gave off a faint but bold blue glow. Goggles rested on her forehead above green eyes that sparkled with excitement, always.

"Addie," Cadena grabbed on to the sleeve of the

Elven woman, "can we stop by the Guildhall? I would enjoy a quiet dinner with you ever so much!"

She had, of all things, a skip in her step, an actual skip in her step. Her tail swishing grew even more excited.

Adelaide rolled her eyes and sighed.

"I suppose I can shift feasting on you for dessert, Lady Reys."

Cadena turned a comically bright red and let go of Adelaide's sleeve, looking now rather sternly at her feet.

"Oh, I wish you would not speak on such things in public, Addie. Everyone in Saint Loras will know about us if you do not mind your mouth!" The anger was feigned.

In truth, no one really seemed to notice them as they walked through the stone streets of the city. Shopkeepers tended to overwhelmingly large flocks of patrons, many of whom were dressed for battle. The pair of women caught the occasional glance of an Avian man or a Arboreal woman, but in all honesty, even the people dancing about on street corners seemed uninterested in the public affection between the Elf and Kitsune.

"Oh, such a scandal that would be!" Adelaide teased. "Can you imagine the whole of the city, nay, the whole of the realm talking about the Lady of Clan Reys and her lascivious knight? The unspeakable acts they engage in with alarming frequency!" She laughed.

It was a boisterous thing a little jarring and a little overdone, but then again so was Adelaide herself.

"And the sex, of course. That as well."

Cadena hit Adelaide's shoulder, braced though it was by the ornamental plate, and smiled up at her.

"My lascivious knight should laugh a little more ladylike!" she teased.

The pair rounded a corner and slipped discreetly past a large group of people chattering away about the dangerous deeds they planned to embark on. It wasn't an unusual thing—the adventurers of the world were its heroes, after all. Everyone sought some of that glory. Even Cadena, who was an engineer by trade, occasionally took Adelaide into ancient and monster dominated ruins to secure rare components for her next gun or airship project.

"In truth, though, I wonder about…possibly…" Cadena's ears drooped slightly and the energy left the swish of her tail. "Could we, perhaps, look at a house of our own? The Residential District is constructing a new subdivision, I hear, and it would be so nice to get away from my family and…and live with you."

"Dena…"

"It's just…you go on missions with the Loras Knights so often and I feel you are ever a world away if you are not in my embrace. We are…we are to be wed, are we not? Should we not have a home of our own, therefore?"

She was sputtering the words quietly as they proceeded down the side street toward the riverfront. She seemed so nervous bringing the topic up.

Adelaide didn't reject the idea, but spoke with hesitance.

"Where would we get the gold? Houses are expensive. Furnishing one triply so. Have you seen what canopy beds alone go for in the carpentry markets?"

She folded her arms, and managed to not waver in her walk even closing her eyes. She knew these streets so well. She'd been, after all, a city guard before becoming a House Knight.

"But if I can take up more assignments for your father and a lot more work for the Loras Knights, and you can start building advanced airship engines fast enough, we can maybe, maybe pull it off."

"My thought exactly!"

Cadena jumped and spun around in front of Adelaide, bringing them both to a stop.

"And you wouldn't have to stay in the barracks in the city, and we could be together each and every night that you aren't on deployment! It would certainly be more personal than saying goodnight by commcrystal! And, um, the…the intimacy."

"Sex."

"That!"

"It's going to be a lot of work, and we're both going to need to put a lot of time into it, doing things we don't really like to do," Adelaide cautioned. "But I think we can get it done. I can even sell my favorite plush, I think it goes for…maybe a million?"

"Your Demon Queen plush? Never! You cuddle her nightly, Addie!" Cadena protested, stomping her foot.

It was Adelaide's turn to be embarrassed.

"Shh, shh, not so loud! I have an image, Dena!"

The rest of the walk to the Guildhall was in relative quiet, Adelaide trying to figure the practicalities of affording a house for the pair of them and Cadena decorating it in her mind. One had been a child of the poor dockworkers of Saint Loras and the other most assuredly had not been, and it showed in their approaches to matters. Cadena never concerned herself with how to afford things, or how much something she wanted cost. She just seized the day. Usually she made up for it with her work as an engineer, but sometimes it was her father bailing her out of debt that made the Kitsune's life comfortable.

Not that Adelaide was marrying into money. She was marrying the love of her life, the woman who gave her a purpose more than following the sword. She loved Cadena. She had loved Cadena since they met, three years ago.

The world was a different place then—recovering from a terrible war with Loras' largest enemies, Tarre and Windcrest. The Three-Nations War had devastated the lands between the nation's defined boundaries, and while the area known now as the Deadlands were a favorite for powerful adventurers, it was a place someone like Cadena really didn't belong. But she'd been there. A dragon elected to make nest in the Deadlands went to find his dinner in the gunsmith, and it was Adelaide who happened upon the scene as part of her reconnaissance for Loras. By working together— Adelaide drawing the dragon's attention and Cadena shooting it at range, they were able to fell the beast. For all they learned that day, the most valuable lesson was how well they moved together, how in perfect harmony they were.

This had led to more adventures, and candlelit dinners, and even to Adelaide joining Cadena at her family's guild, Reys Etheric Engineering as a House Knight. It led to lust. It led to love. It led to a rather sappy proposal at the Singing Waterfalls of Evoral, it led to a night—passionate and writhing and naked— under the stars in the Great Orias Expanse. It led to now. It led to tomorrow, and tomorrow, and tomorrow.

"Ah, Lady Reys, Ser Lumis!" the woman inside

the Guildhall welcomed them with a broad open arms motion. Every time she saw them, it was like she hadn't seen them in years. Or, more accurately, every time she saw them together it was like she hadn't seen them in years. Seeing them apart, she was much less enthused. The receptionist, Rolaine, was far more interested in seeing them together, for whatever reason.

Adelaide sighed and her shoulders slumped. "Please, not 'ser'? I know it's what you call knights, but can't I be, I don't know, Dame Lumis? Or just, maybe, once, you can call me Adelaide like I ask?"

Rolaine grinned widely, with a finger to her chin in fake consideration.

"But shouldn't you be treated with respect for your station, Ser Lumis?"

Rolaine was an Arboreal woman with flowers literally growing from her hair—that's what she elected to call the branches growing on the top of her head. She wore flowing robes that hid most of her figure, and glasses perched on the pale green nose and cheeks of her face put a lens between the world and her honey colored eyes.

The Knight dropped her head in defeat. She knew she wasn't going to win this one.

"Is there a table in the commissary free?"

After leading them back to the near empty commissary and fetching a bit of food for them from whatever happened to be on hand—pineapple juice and fish, it seemed—Rolaine brightly smiled and bowed to them both.

"Have a good dinner, ladies!" she chirped.

And then she dashed out of the room. Of course, Adelaide and Cadena were sure she was standing right on the other side of the door listening to them, it was something of a pattern for Rolaine, but they didn't much mind. They were used to it at this point.

"So, about the wedding," Adelaide broke the quiet that settled after Rolaine's departure.

"I was thinking we take everyone to the Cathedral of the Crystal on one of your airships, and we have the reception in the air on the return journey? I mean, since we have to fly to and from the Floating City anyway, right?"

Cadena shoved a forkful of grilled trout into her mouth and made a little approving sound, both at the food and the idea.

"I'm not sure how much work it would take to put an open bar on an airship, but I will certainly direct the Reys Corps of Engineers to work that one out!" She followed the fish with a swig of pineapple juice, which she hadn't anticipated being a good combination but fell squarely into the not displeasing category.

She smiled and offered a slight nod. "You think once we're married Rol will start calling me Lady instead of Ser?"

From outside the room came the voice of the spying Rolaine.

"Absolutely not, Ser Lumis!" Rolaine shouted.

"Absolutely not, Addie," echoed Cadena with a laugh.

The pout on Adelaide's face was less an expression and more a state of being.

In an effort to bring a smile to her fiancée, Cadena reached across the table and stuck her fork right in Adelaide's mouth, a bit of grilled fish being forced into the knight's pouting face. That did earn a smile, one that wasn't just the product of surprised chewing but a grateful expression.

As amusing as Rolaine's antics were, sometimes they made Adelaide feel as though she couldn't be all at once a brave knight, attracted to other women and still feminine. She often had concern that she could only be two of those three things. While the expectation that this ought to be true wasn't malicious on the part of people like Rolaine, it felt so constraining. It felt like being strangled by a Kraken or tentacled hellbeast. Cadena never made her feel that way.

One more reason she loved the shipwright.

In return, Adelaide never questioned why a daughter of nobility liked to dress like a male sky pirate, especially when Cadena was one of the most downright girly people she knew. The Kitsune was bouncy and cute and soft to the touch. She got flustered by Adelaide's comfort with topics like sexuality and was totally enthralled with notions of romance and princesses in shining armor. She was brave, and foolish and silly. She wasn't a picture of what people expected either. Maybe that's why they saw one another as people, and not as expectations. Maybe it's why there was such respect for the ways they deviated from, what was seen as usual, in a world that loved the extraordinary of skill and scorned the extraordinary of style.

A few men and women wandered through the commissary as the betrothed couple ate in a cordial and intimate quiet. Most of them collected their food and left, rather than staying to eat. Those that did stay mostly milled about one another, ignoring Cadena and Adelaide. It made the moment slightly more awkward, but only marginally so, as they were used to Rolaine's well-intentioned interference around the Guildhall. Some little chatter around them was loud enough to pick up. Something about an ancient monster roaming a bitterly cold island north of Windcrest. Something about a chance to race one of the new pinnaces the engineers were building—that story got a glance from Cadena but she decided not to join their conversation. Something about their wedding—seemed a little rude to discuss their wedding as if they weren't there, but that was the nature of life, Adelaide supposed.

"Should we go somewhere more private?" Cadena suggested, noticing a bit of tension in Adelaide's posture. "Or we can take in a show at the Caged Bird Cabaret?"

The Knight dabbed her mouth with a cloth and set it beside her now empty plate. "Somewhere private, I think. Your office?" she posed, trying to smile.

Too much was on her mind right now, she needed something to cut through the clutter. Something tender. Love. Love would cut through the clutter.

With a nod, the Kitsune rose to her feet, offering her hand to the much taller Elf woman. Adelaide took it, and let Cadena help her to her feet before they walked out of the room, this time with Cadena leading the way.

"I forget sometimes you have trouble focusing when it gets too noisy," Cadena offered apologetically.

Adelaide shook her head, "No, no, it's nothing. Don't worry about it," she followed close, but didn't overtake her partner.

If Cadena had chosen to take the lead, it was Cadena who would lead. That was vone of the balances of their relationship. Everything was in flux—everything changed and yet—was still always the same. They switched off roles to one another as easily as they would switch from one weapon to the next. It was an almost effortless transition.

Cadena's office was a beautiful place. There was an ornate desk with schematics of airships on the wall all around it, and a massive painting on one wall showed a large, proud dreadnaught with Loras' colors draped across it. A name emblazoned on one of the bold blue banners proclaimed its name as the LSF Siege Perilous. It was a proud damned ship, and clearly Cadena was proud of her role in building it. There were models of ships everywhere in the room, some hanging from the ceiling and acting as lamps and others sitting on shelves along the walls. Along the back wall, where natural light poured in from the sun setting outside windows, were large easels and chalkboards with schematics on them. The blue and white banner of Loras hung behind her desk. It absolutely looked like a shipwright's workspace, and one belonging to an engineer of renown.

Beat the hell out of Adelaide's barracks.

As the door behind Adelaide closed itself—another mechanical creation of Cadena's making it happen—another of those subtle but powerful transitions in the interaction between the partners took place. In this private space, a glint of need shimmered in Cadena's eyes.

Her mouth was a little dry when she spoke, and it seemed to take a lot of inner strength for her to make such a bold statement as this, but it had been on her mind for tolls and tolls now, since it was first mentioned on their walk.

"I, uh, I thought you might like…dessert?"

She leaned back against her desk, mostly to steady herself but also because she thought it made her back bend in a way Adelaide might find pleasing to see.

Adelaide was thankful for two things at the moment. First, she was thankful the walls were sound-proof enough that she was reasonably sure that Rolaine wasn't going to be listening outside. Second, it was a wonderful thing that her light parade armor was little more than a nice jacket with plate on the shoulders. The armor was easy to shed, and it easily clanked to the floor, leaving her in the camisole she wore beneath it and the trousers that matched it. "I am still hungry," she admitted playfully.

The feeling of the Elvan woman's lips on hers, of her body pressing promisingly against Cadena's, made the engineer close her eyes and fall back onto the desk, having lost interest in supporting her own weight—documents, drawings, writing implements all went falling around them to the floor, and neither woman cared a single tick about it. Even the model of the Siege Perilous on her desk was made of stern enough stuff to weather a fall to the ground. Rigorous testing like this over the years had proven as much.

Three years on, it still felt like a fire inside them both. The times they were alone, together, were increasingly rare as their duties demanded more and more of them. It helped the spark of need to burst into a mighty flame when they could be together, and a fire that would burn all through the night without cessation or diminishing return, if patterns held true.

This kiss, this touch, this was all a promise of a thousand nights like this, a thousand sunsets and sunrises met both in the throes of passion. If a picture spoke countless words, this kiss spoke countless emotions and dreams and hopes. And soon they'd be married, and that kiss, too, would promise the world to them.

And then something strange happened. The kiss

stopped. Cadena was gone.

"Fuck!" screamed a woman's voice in Jasmine's ear. She winced and leaned away from the sound as if she could actually get away from it, but since it was coming through her headset she really had no escape.

Jasmine let out a small, slow sigh.

"Ping timeout?"

The woman on the other end, Max, grumbled back.

"That's, what, the fifth time this week? And right as it was getting hot!"

Jasmine slumped her shoulders. She quickly ran a hand through her hair, unlike her Elvan avatar Jasmine's was brown and barely shoulder-length. It was in need of a good comb. She'd been wearing her headset for about five hours now and it showed. She didn't even notice the collections of strands caught in the joints of one of her earpieces. The room around her was dark, but illuminated by the screen where a now half naked Knight of Loras was standing next to an empty desk.

"You should contact your ISP, honey," she said with a shallow breath. She had to calm herself a little. She was getting so worked up by the writing. More so than she'd have wanted to admit to anyone but Max.

"It's not just this game either, right? It's happening in Laniakea too, isn't it?"

"Yeah," Max's voice responded. "VOIP calls still seem to work though."

Jasmine ran her hand down her collarbone, realized she was doing it and stopped herself.

"Want to log back in or continue here on call?"

They'd done both in situations like this before. Another thing Jasmine didn't want to admit was how much she loved talking to Max in character. It was a weird thing, but it was how they had met, and there was something about embracing that which felt so lovely to Jasmine.

It was how they handled the distance. Thousands of miles separated them in the physical world. It made things like dates exceedingly hard to manage. And while they had visited one another more than once, and seen one another's cities, and been at one another's favorite restaurants and parks and hangouts, it was the game that was their date spot and their avatars that brought their relationship to life. The game eliminated the distance, it let them tell a version of their story that was, although different in every way, somehow more physical and personal.

It wasn't like their characters were just themselves in a fantasy world. Jasmine was anything other than a brave hero, and Max wasn't so much an engineer as she was a stocker at a grocery store. But these proxies, Adelaide and Cadena, these other people that they wrote and controlled—this was a way to live vicariously through them.

It also meant connection problems were date-killers.

"I think I'm going to try to reset my router," Max replied with an angry grumble.

Jasmine quickly interrupted.

"Honey, also maybe take an anxiety pill? You sound really tense."

There was a silence on the call. Jasmine went to check to make sure it hadn't dropped and that Max was still on it. She was. Good.

"Honey?"

There was a shuffle on the other end and Max

responded.

"It's been a rough week, you know?"

"I know," Jasmine responded. "I wish I could be there to hold you, make you something to eat."

That earned a laugh from Max.

"You burned water once. You set water on your stove and the smoke alarms went off."

"I should've never told you that story, I'm never going to live it down."

"Maybe," Max admitted, "but the laugh was nice. Be right back."

The call ended.

Jasmine looked at the little cartoon style drawing of Cadena on her screen, wishing it would be ringed in green again to indicate the call was back on. Some people, especially her family, didn't understand how she could date a woman from so far away. Plane tickets don't grow on trees. Did this mean Jasmine was going to move far away to be with Max? Was Max going to uproot her life and move here? And when? Shouldn't this have been made real years ago?

It was real now. It wasn't physical, but with their love of roleplaying, especially erotic roleplaying, it didn't feel like they were a world apart. They were on a call together most of the day, every day. They were constantly with one another in every way other than physical. And yeah, that hurt. Hell, it burned at times like this. Jasmine was worried and sexually frustrated. The failed connection could potentially be the straw to break her strained emotional state and leave her sobbing. That didn't make it less real.

It felt like it took hours, but her system clock assured her it was only a few minutes when the circle lit green again.

"Am I back?" came Max's voice.

"Yup, I hear you," responded Jasmine, trying to hide the smile on her face from her voice.

There was the sound of a sharp intake of breath and a few keystrokes on the other end of the call.

"Logging back in now."

"Hey, Maxie?"

Jasmine didn't even let Max finish talking before trying to hold her attention. It was a gently prying tone. She was trying to get some focus without it sounding like there was a problem or issue. This elicited a sound of interest from Max, though not concern. The little sound from across the country made Jasmine smile, it filled her with warmth and made the words she meant to say all that much easier. It was natural. It was something that, by giving it voice, made everything better for Jasmine. She thought, that the words made everything better for Max too. She hoped. She believed.

"I love you."

"I love you too, Jazz."

That made the smile wide enough that she couldn't keep the happiness from her tone. She might've even giggled, though there was no way she'd ever admit to it. She fancied herself too cool for that kind of thing. Though, being honest with herself, she was fine being that vulnerable with Max.

Things weren't perfect, or even ideal, but Jasmine felt that doing what she could, gentle reminders of caring in hard times and some cute or hot roleplaying over online games, made a difference. She could hear it in Max's voice. She saw it when they video-called. She hoped. She believed.

"Oh, hey, you're back in! Want me to resend my last turn?" she asked, the happiness evident in her voice.

"Yeah, could you?"

This kiss, this touch, this was all a promise of a thousand nights like this, a thousand sunsets and sunrises met both in the throes of passion. If a picture could speak countless words, this kiss spoke countless emotions and dreams and hopes. And soon they'd be married, and that kiss, too, would promise the world to them.

And, in it's own way—in their own time—the kiss promised as much for their players as it did for the characters. Love, both beyond and outside the screens, tied them together and promised that well beyond the last expansion of the game Adelaide and Cadena would be together, would grow old together and would raise children together through some contrived story element or plot device with no meaning other than to allow them to do as they wished—and that same promise was what Jasmine and Max believed in as well.

Katelyn is an author and journalist from Kalamazoo, Michigan and graduate of Western Michigan University who enjoys all things nerdy. As an author, Katelyn dabbles in lesbian-centric science fiction and fantasy, as well as online collaborative writing. Yes, she role-plays in online games.

Geekily Yours

By Samantha Luce

*T*he *Annihilator* was a short-lived sci-fi TV show I fell in love with a couple years ago. Aliens, robots, and kickass women, oh my! It was a little slice of heaven. When the network cancelled it on a cliffhanger I was heartbroken. I signed up for every petition I could find to save the show, but no luck. We didn't get another season. No movie to wrap it all up or even a limited run comic book to give us fans some much needed closure. I had to be content with using a screenshot as my computer background and re-watching the DVDs on my own. Or did I?

Turns out I did have another option. I found out when my computer had a massive glitch at work. The tried and true, turn it off, let it rest, then turn it back on method failed me. My stomach twisted. The last time I'd had to deal with one of the IT guys he'd made me feel like a complete idiot. Every question he asked me, stumped me. *When's the last time you defragged? Did you do a warm or cold reboot? Have you cleared your cookies lately?* It was like he was speaking a foreign language.

I cringed at the memory. If not for my fast approaching deadline I don't think I would've found the courage to dial the extension for IT. A gruff male voice answered. I gave him my name and started to describe the issue. He cut me off with a loud sigh.

"Never mind. I'll send someone." He grumbled and hung up.

I expected a long wait. I opened my office door, on my way to the coffeemaker, and almost collided with a petite brunette in a Guns N Roses T-shirt, skinny jeans, and knee high, black boots with buckles from ankle to knee. Her caramel skin was flawless. She had big brown eyes surrounded by thick, dark lashes and a generous smile.

"Hi," she held out her hand. "I'm Oz. Are you Stephanie?"

I nodded and shook her hand. The warmth of her skin and the pleasant scent of a body wash or light perfume caught me off guard. Instant attraction isn't a sensation I'm used to feeling. It took me a moment before I regained my senses and took a step backward so she could enter the office.

She walked over to the computer and began moving the mouse.

"Oh, wow." Her heart shaped face lit up when she smiled. "*The Annihilator*. Great show. I've written some fanfic for it."

"Fanfic?" My eyebrow arched.

"Yeah," her smile faltered and her apple cheeks darkened. "Sorry, I'm such a dork for everything sci-fi. It's this crazy thing a lot of us fans do. We write continuations or alternate universe stories about our favorite shows and we share them on the internet."

"You're kidding."

"Nope. It's true." With a few keystrokes the screen switched to an old black and white script style I remembered from my very first interactions with computers.

I sat on the edge of my desk and watched her nimble fingers flying over the keys. The screen flashed and blinked. She shook her head, the springy coils of her dark brown hair bouncing with even the slightest movement. She typed some more and the color came back on the screen. It was like watching a magician. I couldn't wait to see what her next trick would be.

A few minutes later she rolled back in the chair.

"I'm running a few things to clean your system. It might take a little while."

"So, tell me more about this fanfic."

She rolled her eyes.

"Don't get me started. I might not ever shut up."

"I'm not complaining." I hoped my smile was as inviting as hers.

I suppose it was. We spent the next forty minutes discussing the best episodes and this whole new world of stories about the characters we loved while she worked her charms on my computer and me.

"You're all set, Stephanie. It was nice meeting you and talking about *The Annihalator*. I miss it so much."

"Me too." I held up the card she'd given me with all the fan fiction links on it. "I'm looking forward to reading these stories, especially those you wrote. Maybe I'll run into you at the coffee machine sometime and we can talk about it."

Her carefree expression faltered.

"Not unless you have a teleportation machine, which would be awesome. You don't have one of those do you?"

"I'm afraid not." I laughed. "It is on my wish list though."

She laughed with me.

"That's a shame. Today was my last day of training here in this office. I'm transferring to the Florida office on Monday."

"Oh." I hoped my disappointment wasn't stamped across my forehead. In my head I'd already pictured us becoming friends and who knows what after that.

"Well, thank you for everything, Oz. Best of luck in the new office."

She held up her right hand in the salute made famous by the beautiful assassin from our show.

"It's weird. I know we just met, but I feel like we're close. Must be the kindred spirit thing. Anyway, my email and cell are on the other side of that card. I'd really like you to keep in touch."

"Count on it." I said.

❧❧❧❧

I didn't know if Oz was named after the wizard or not, but she was definitely magical. After I got home I couldn't wait to dive into the sites she'd shared with me. I started hopping from one page to the next while I ate my salad. Oz's links opened my eyes to a brand new world filled with all my favorite characters. This was a fresh landscape for people I cared for, and the best part, in this realm there were no censors. No restrictions on the imagination. It was a virtual playground where any and every character could mix and match. People could be gay, straight, funny, serious, or just totally random from one scene to the next. I won't lie. There were some bad stories that were poorly written and barely researched, but there were also stories that were as good as the ones I'd watched week after week.

Oz had written over a dozen stories based on *The Annihilator*. I skimmed the ones written by others while I ate, but I wanted to savor Oz's. I selected one that continued where the unresolved cliffhanger had left off, uploaded it to my e-reader and tucked myself into bed with a tall glass of wine.

It was close to midnight when I'd finished her novella. My emotions had been on one hell of a rollercoaster ride. I picked up my cellphone and debated a text or an email. Not knowing if I'd wake her or possibly interrupt a date I opted for an email.

Hi Oz,

I'm so glad we met today. I can't thank you enough for giving me the links to my new favorite addiction. I just finished, *Carry On*. It was everything I hoped for on the series and then some. You have a gift with words and character emotion. The show writers made the tension between Andrea and Peyton palpable. I thought it was just me and my overactive imagination that sometimes it seemed their animosity was mixed with a touch of grudging admiration and desire. You picked up on it too and managed to realistically make their lust/hate relationship believable and steamy. I'm looking forward to reading your other stories soon. Hope the move goes well.

Best to you,
Steph

On impulse I added my phone number and hit send before I could chicken out. I didn't expect a reply right away. I thought maybe she'd send a quick thank you the next time she logged on. No big deal. The chirp coming from my cell just a minute or so later had to be a random coincidence. I snatched up the phone and hoped the butterflies in my stomach would go back to sleep. There was a text from a number my phone didn't recognize.

"Still awake? Want to talk?"

Before I could think too much about it I typed back yes to both.

I answered before the ringtone even started. I knew she couldn't see me, but I pulled off my glasses and fluffed my hair anyway.

Her soft-spoken greeting was like a caress against my ear.

"You don't know what a relief it is to hear that you liked the story, Steph. I've been kicking myself all day. I totally forgot to tell you about the lesbian relationship. Glad I didn't scare you off."

I chuckled as the warmth rose to my cheeks.

"No. Definitely didn't scare me. Might have done something else to me."

Oh God. Did I really just say that out loud? It must have been the wine and us not being able to see each other that made me so bold.

"Whoa, girl." She laughed. "You are something else. Why the hell didn't we meet sooner?"

"Yeah," I sighed. "Tell me about it. We could be curled up watching *The Annihilator* right now."

"We still can."

"What?" I sat up straight, glancing at my comfortable but unflattering flannel pajamas. Panic set in. "Are you still in town?"

"I wish."

Her warm laughter against my ear made a chill race along my spine.

"But we could still watch a show. I have the series on my computer and I bet you've got the DVDs, right?"

"Absolutely. What've you got planned?"

"Keep the phone lines open, sync up our players and hit play."

❧ ❧ ❧ ❧

It worked too. For that first night and just about every night after for the next 4 months we dated via phone and computer. We watched the complete series and quite a few more after that with movies sprinkled in here and there. Five states and a mountain of snow separated us, but we still found ways to get closer. Not seeing each other in the flesh was doing wonders for my confidence. I said things I'd never have the courage to say to anyone's face. I did a few things too.

Oz had an incredible imagination and a true gift with words. I came more often and harder with her whispering in my ear through a cell phone than I did with some people I'd dated in person.

And now it was time to see her for real. The plane I'd been scared to get on at first had finally landed. Now it was time to get off and I was hanging on to the armrests. The butterflies I'd started this trip with had been kicked out or drowned in stomach acid. Wicked wasps had taken their place, flitting around and making my abdominal walls spasm. Tiny drops of perspiration collected on my upper lip. My legs were weak. Not just my legs, every part of me seemed fragile, when I stood.

The Comic-Con with our two favorite leading ladies from *The Annihilator* didn't start until Friday. That gave Oz and I today and tomorrow to get to know each other while in the same room.

Will she be as magical in person? Will I be a stuttering, shy, dork? Will our conversations flow as naturally? Is the fantasy us better than the real us? Will she still want to be with me? Can she live up to the hype? Will I still want her to try?

The shuffling crowd urged me forward to the exit. I clutched my carry-on bag tighter…my eyes flitting in every direction.

Soft hands clasped my shoulders from behind. Before the panic could get a stronger hold, a scent drifted toward my nose, warm vanilla cookies. I turned around and the air stopped. Everything melted into a sea of things I cared nothing about. Everything with the exception of the brown eyed woman with the smile that managed to be shy, confident, and terribly sexy all at once.

"Steph," she squealed and enveloped me in a crushing hug.

Her fingers rubbing up and down my back. It was what she did next that made all the angry wasps quiet. She brought her face close to my neck and breathed in deeply, her hand came forward and she cupped my cheek…her thumb slowly caressing until she reached the corner of my mouth.

"You're more beautiful today than you were on the day we met."

Someone bumped into me from behind and I wound up breast to breast with Oz pressed firmly against the wall. Her easy laughter teased my ears.

"I guess you missed me too, huh?"

"I did." I laughed too. "But this wasn't my fault. Some clumsy jerk just about knocked me over."

"It doesn't matter." She took my hand and brought it to her soft lips. "The only thing that matters is you're finally here. Let's get your luggage and get you home."

Home, I repeated to myself. I liked the sound of that.

The airport was huge. Hundreds or maybe thousands of people milling about, some in a rush, others barely trudging along. If I'd been alone I probably would have found a corner to hide in for at least a few minutes to calm the fluttering wasps and get my bearings. With Oz, I didn't need that quiet time. Some of her confidence seemed to have seeped under my skin.

We collected my bags and she led me outside to the unexpectedly empty parking garage. Her neon green Eco friendly car was in a row all by itself. It was compact and cute, just like its owner. She helped me stow my bags in the trunk and surprised me with another hug.

I lingered in her embrace, standing in the underground garage, enjoying her warm welcome. Her eyes held mine. I saw nothing but desire and friendship in their depths. I cradled her face in my hands. My thumbs tracing all the places I wanted so desperately to kiss. Her wine colored lipstick was enticing me to lick it. I grinned and gently ran my thumb along the length of her smile.

Just as I fought the temptation and was ready to pull away she leaned forward. Soft, moist lips met mine. I moaned at the first contact. She tasted like cherry. I inhaled deeply. The combined scents of cherry and vanilla on her dark skin had my mouth watering.

Moments later her lips parted. Her wet tongue slid over my lips. It was a sexy move, one she'd whispered in my ear during phone interludes in my room. I'd dreamt about it and now I was feeling it.

"Damn, Oz, you're killing me. Take me home," I murmured against her mouth. "Now."

She took my hand and led me to the passenger door. She held the door as I got in and I caught her looking at my legs.

"Thank you for wearing the dress," she said. Color rose on her plump cheeks and she looked the tiniest bit unsure.

"Did you wear the other things?"

I understood then that it wasn't the anonymity of the phone that emboldened me. It was she. I grasped the hem of my skirt and slowly raised it until the garter straps showed.

Her dark eyes opened wider. I doubt she even realized she was licking her lips, but I noticed.

"Get your ass in the car and drive, Oz," I teased her.

I won't swear to it, but I think she might have sped a little once we hit the freeway. I'd never been to Florida before. I probably should have been trying to take in the sights. I couldn't take my eyes off her.

We reached her apartment about thirty minutes later and hastily grabbed my bags and dragged them inside. I started to say something about how nice the apartment was, but she stopped me with a searing kiss. Her hands grasped my hips and she pushed me against the wall. The urgency of her frantic movements allowed me to sense her raw need. It matched my own.

I liked the tingle that spread from just above my ass to the base of my neck. I drew her closer with one hand low on her hip and the other around the back of her neck. The kiss deepened as we freely explored each other.

"I'm so sorry," she whispered after a while. "I'm ravishing you. I haven't let you get settled or…"

I brought my finger to her lips.

"It's all good." I peppered her neck with kisses. "Does it look like I'm complaining?"

"But, I'm being a bad host. Do you want a drink? Are you hungry?" she asked, her voice soft and breathy.

"Oh yeah," Desire had my own voice sounding deeper. "I'm hungry, Oz." I gave her another kiss. "But only for you." My lips grazed her from her collarbone to back behind her ear. She tasted sweet.

She trembled, leaning her head back to give me better access. Her breath quickened when her hands came up to cup my breasts. A steady heat built between my legs as we explored with fingers and tongues.

At some point she clasped my hand in hers and began nudging me backward. Thankfully, the bedroom was close by. I didn't get a chance to admire it much before she had me on the bed. It was a modest queen with a fluffy flannel comforter. It felt divine. Soft, warm, and welcoming, just like Oz.

Her shirt hit the floor and I was treated to her beautiful breasts encased in white lace. She reached behind her and unclasped the lacy bra in a heartbeat. Her dark nipples were hard and pointing right at me. She gave me a slow smile and reached for the button on her jeans.

My tongue swept across my lips. Her eyes never left mine. I leaned back and enjoyed her unhurried striptease. It was clear she worked out. My heart pounded hard in my chest.

"C'mere," I whispered when she was completely nude.

"I want to taste you."

"Not yet." She wagged her finger at me.

"First, I have to see you."

I sat up and started to reach for the zipper at the back of my neck, but she caught my wrist in her hand. She motioned for me to roll over onto my stomach. I smiled and complied.

She straddled my waist and laid her body on top of mine. Her teeth settled on my zipper. Her breath tickled me as she slowly eased the full-length zipper down. Her fingers stroked my skin as she uncovered it.

I wriggled and moaned. The deliberate slowness of her moves kept me hovering at the edge.

She spent some time feeling my stocking clad legs before climbing back up and biting the band at the top of my underwear. Now I understood why she'd wanted me to wear the panties over the garter straps. It had seemed an odd request until I realized it meant she could remove them and I could keep the stockings and garter on for her pleasure.

I raised my hips when she started to pull, allowing her to drag the panties down and off. My fingers tightened and twisted the comforter. My heartbeat and her breathing the only sounds I could focus on. Both were speeding.

She settled low on my hips. Those graceful fingers of hers landed on my shoulders, kneading and teasing as she worked her way down. The clasp of my bra unhooked in short order.

"God, you feel good," she whispered, leaning forward and draping her body over mine.

I resisted and tried to rise up. I couldn't take it anymore. I needed to see her, had to touch her, and was positively overwhelmed with the burning desire to taste her.

"Damn, girl. You look like an angel, but you buck like the devil." She laughed softly and rolled off me.

I laughed too. "You weren't playing fair."

"You're too pretty to argue with." She grinned and shifted onto her back.

"I'm all yours. Do whatever you want."

I leaned down and kissed her...my tongue stroking hers. My fingers skimmed over her torso, delighting in every tightened muscle and flutter of skin. I worked my way lower, kissing and licking wherever my fingers had made her react strongly.

"Oh, sweet Jesus, you're killing me," she said and grasped my hair. "I love your long hair. Brush it against me."

I did exactly as she requested, reveling at the tremors and soft giggles each brief touch elicited.

"Every night we talked on the phone I dreamed about you doing this."

"Oh," I looked up and smirked. I made sure she was focused on my eyes and quickly brought my fingers to her hot mound.

"What about this?"

"Oh, God yes."

"Good." I lowered my head and sucked a hardened nipple into my mouth. My fingers found her wetness, dipping and tickling until her strong thighs clenched my hand.

Her hands wound through my hair, guiding my lips where she wanted them. Soft moans spurred me on. The pressure from her thighs let up and I continued exploring her treasure with the tips of my fingers.

I slipped lower until I was breathing in the pure essence of Oz. My tongue drifted lazily along her underwear line. She was as wet as I was. I kissed the inside of her thigh, swirling my tongue against her hot flesh, making her whimper. I nibbled when I reached the skin between the top of her thigh and pussy. Her deep moan and a full body shiver was my reward.

I spread her open with my thumbs. Her moist pink center beckoned. I inhaled deeply and brought my flattened tongue against her.

Her hips rose, strong hands back in my hair and pressing me tightly to her. She was mumbling. I couldn't make out much except for the occasional curse.

I wrapped my arms around her legs, sucking and kissing all her secret places while she rocked her hips side to side and up and down. I slowed down. She squeezed tighter. Her grip on my hair verged on painful until I resumed sucking her clit. Moments later her back arched, thighs clenched, hips slammed upward, and she let out a growl when she came.

I held her until the tremors stopped, kissed each of her slick thighs and slid higher until I could kiss her mouth. She kissed me back. Her tongue insistent in it's questing.

I thought she might need to rest. I'm happy to admit I was wrong. Her open mouth was wet and hot as it glided lower along my skin. Her knee demanded a place between my thighs.

My already puckered nipples hardened to almost painful points when she began to suck and play. She'd kiss each nipple lightly, meet my gaze briefly and bite down at the same time her knee would press harder between my legs.

Fire spread from my center through every limb as she teased. Her lips and fingers kept me on the edge so long I was afraid I'd pass out.

She must have picked up on a change in my breathing or movements. She finally relented and narrowed her focus to where I needed it most. Fingers twisted and buried deep inside me while her talented tongue conquered my clit.

We lay together for a while, her half draped across my waist. Our sweat slicked arms and legs tangled together.

When coherent thoughts returned to my brain I collected her in my arms and gave her a soft kiss. I gently nibbled her bottom lip.

"You're fucking amazing, Oz."

"The feeling is mutual, babe." She leaned across me and reached into the nightstand drawer, retrieving a packet of papers.

"You don't have to commit. I'm happy with whatever you want to offer, but I printed these transfer papers out. I have plenty of room in my apartment or it just so happens there's a vacancy in the building and you could get your own place if you're afraid I'm bringing up the U-Haul too quickly."

I laughed at the hint of a stupid U-Haul joke.

"Hold that thought," I said and hurried back to the doorway where we'd left my luggage. I grabbed the manila envelope and brought it back to her.

"Great minds really do think alike. You make me so happy. You've annihilated my heart."

She groaned at my lame show reference, but smiled when she saw the same transfer paperwork already printed and filled in. She pulled me to her and gave me a quick peck on the lips, before backing away. She gave me the Annihilator salute...her expression suddenly very somber.

"I don't think anyone else could handle our bad

jokes and puns. If you'll have me, I'm geekily yours."

Samantha Luce loves erotica. She enjoys writing it, reading it, and of course, "researching it." Her long distance love lives in Wisconsin. Their mutual fear of flying and a mountain of snow conspire to keep them apart, but they're working on bridging the gap.

Now that you've enjoyed Volume Two in a Heart Well Traveled Anthology Series, be sure to pick up your copy of Volumes One and Three.

**A Heart Well Traveled
Volume One
Tales of Long Distance Love Affairs and Unlikely Outcomes**

Discover the many facets of romantic relationships as authors in Volume One of, *A Heart Well Traveled*, unravel the trials and tribulations of long distance love affairs.

Each author, with their own unique style of storytelling, will leave the reader begging for more. Go from wild rides to gentle love stories, exploring the twists and turns lovers go through as they work to be together despite the distance between them.

Explore bonds beyond friendship, chance meetings, family drama, gender complexity, longstanding love and unexpected passion as lovers seek their happily ever after.

A Heart Well Traveled is a collection of short stories where women who love woman share the joys and challenges of long distance relationships.

Can love really conquer all?

Coming December 2017

A Heart Well Traveled

Volume Three
Tales of Long Distance Love Affairs and Unlikely Outcomes

Love stretches across international boundaries as Sapphire brings you a collection of unique stories of romance and intrigue across the continents.

Pack your bags and let your imagination run wild as you find yourself on romantic escapes to Africa, Australia, Bora Bora, Canada, Europe, the Middle East, South America and the United Kingdom.

This fast-paced anthology will leave you wondering if you could endure love with nothing but miles between you and your lover. Watch as the characters face countless impossibilities without ever losing sight of the one thing we all want, one true love.

Can they defy the odds?

Other Anthologies by Sapphire Books Publishing

The One: Stories of Falling in Love Forever - ISBN - 978-1-943353-32-3

If lucky enough, we fall in love once in a lifetime.

Children's books and romance novels promise us an encounter with a beautiful, mythical love – a passionate lover that sweeps us off kilter and changes everyday life into happily-ever-after. In reality, most fall in love a couple of times throughout a lifetime. Yet, those relationships fail to fulfill the "forever" expectancy – they end. Still, we hope that love, true and eternal will embrace us. We hope that stardust will cover the banal when life becomes monotonous or loneliness grasps us too firmly when days fades to night.

Reading about love triumphant sparks desire for more than uninspired routine existence.

In *The One*, an assortment of writers chronicle the discovery of the one woman to share the rest of life's journey.

Everyone deserves happily ever after!

A Sapphire Collection - Our Stories Continue Vol. 1 - ISBN - 978-1-943353-49-1

We craft lives from memories, shared moments with others, and from our experience as beings in the world. Our stories emerge from fashioning bits and pieces of life together with imagination and putting these ideas into words. As writers, we build worlds, give birth to characters, and hope to create a portal into a new realm, a place of communion of ideas, where fiction is alive in the mind of the reader. That's the joy of having others read our work. Our stories continue in the mind of the reader. Stories become shared spaces of strength, joy, personal insight, and where the individual loses herself for a while in an alternative realm of her own creation.

www.ingramcontent.com/pod-product-compliance
Lightning Source LLC
Chambersburg PA
CBHW050352190726

48284CB00007BB/2249